EIGHT MAIDS A MILKING

Twelve Days of Christmas

Emily E K Murdoch

ARE YOU SIGNED UP FOR DRAGONBLADE'S BLOG?

You'll get the latest news and information on exclusive giveaways, exclusive excerpts, coming releases, sales, free books, cover reveals and more.

Check out our complete list of authors, too!

No spam, no junk. That's a promise!

Sign Up Here

www.dragonbladepublishing.com

Dearest Reader;

Thank you for your support of a small press. At Dragonblade Publishing, we strive to bring you the highest quality Historical Romance from some of the best authors in the business. Without your support, there is no 'us', so we sincerely hope you adore these stories and find some new favorite authors along the way.

Happy Reading!

CEO, Dragonblade Publishing

Additional Dragonblade books by Author Emily E K Murdoch

Twelve Days of Christmas
Twelve Drummers Drumming
Eleven Pipers Piping
Ten Lords a Leaping
Nine Ladies Dancing
Eight Maids a Milking
Seven Swans a Swimming
Six Geese a Laying

The De Petras Saga
The Misplaced Husband (Book 1)
The Impoverished Dowry (Book 2)
The Contrary Debutante (Book 3)
The Determined Mistress (Book 4)
The Convenient Engagement (Book 5)

The Governess Bureau Series
A Governess of Great Talents (Book 1)
A Governess of Discretion (Book 2)
A Governess of Many Languages (Book 3)
A Governess of Prodigious Skill (Book 4)
A Governess of Unusual Experience (Book 5)
A Governess of Wise Years (Book 6)
A Governess of No Fear (Novella)

Never The Bride Series
Always the Bridesmaid (Book 1)
Always the Chaperone (Book 2)
Always the Courtesan (Book 3)

Always the Best Friend (Book 4)
Always the Wallflower (Book 5)
Always the Bluestocking (Book 6)
Always the Rival (Book 7)
Always the Matchmaker (Book 8)
Always the Widow (Book 9)
Always the Rebel (Book 10)
Always the Mistress (Book 11)
Always the Second Choice (Book 12)
Always the Mistletoe (Novella)
Always the Reverend (Novella)

The Lyon's Den Series
Always the Lyon Tamer

Pirates of Britannia Series
Always the High Seas

De Wolfe Pack: The Series
Whirlwind with a Wolfe

Selina and Arthur and Dorothea
Caroline
Arabella
Sophia
Esther
Lucy
Jemima
London
Rupert and Frances
Joy
Harmony
William and Leonora
Olivia
Katarina
Isabella
Maria
Bath
Chalcroft
Fitzroy

CHAPTER ONE

I F KATARINA FITZROY had her way, of course, she would not even be in the great hall of Chalcroft to welcome everyone in the first place.

"Don't push me!"

"Careful with that bag, it has my favorite gown—"

"Oh, the decorations look marvelous!"

"Well, Chalcroft always looks its best at Christmas…"

Standing at the very end of the corridor, just out of sight of her sister Olivia who was peering down at the minstrels' gallery, Katarina sighed heavily and knew there was nothing for it. She had no choice. Her mother had made her promise—and once Leonora determined something, all four of her daughters were forced to obey.

It may be fathers in many families who ruled the roost, but Katarina—or Kitty, to her siblings—had always known their mother was the one with the real power, and she had been very direct at breakfast that morning.

"Your cousins are coming to Chalcroft for Christmas," she had said, glaring over the breakfast table. "And I expect all of you—*all of you*, Maria—to welcome them."

Isabella and Olivia had demurred and agreed, of course, Katarina thought viciously as she watched her cousins arrive at a distance. Maria had managed to hide away—the youngest sister was shy, true, but because she was the baby of the family, she managed to get away with murder.

And that left only one other sibling. *Her.*

"Oh, Chalcroft, you never change," said one of her cousins, Jemima. "If only Caroline could be here, she loves it at Christmas."

"She will give birth any moment, Jemmy, you know there was no possibility of her traveling," snapped her sister Esther. "Really, it's not all about you!"

"I did not say it was," Jemima retorted loudly.

Katarina crept along the corridor toward Olivia, who had not yet noticed her, transfixed as she was at the spectacle of their family arriving.

Why it was so fascinating, Katarina could not say. Their father had two brothers, and they all had daughters. There were twelve Fitzroy cousins in total, and although not every one of them had made it to Chalcroft for Christmas this year, there were a good number of people down there.

Katarina glanced over the banister, then drew back hastily in case she was spotted. Harmony, in particular—one of her cousins from Bath—had very fine sight. Thankfully, she was predominately hidden by the Christmas decorations the servants had spent far too much time on, in her opinion.

Not that anyone had listened to her, of course.

As it happened, however, though Katarina would be loath to admit it to anyone, the festoons of ivy in the garlands along the top banister were rather convenient. They allowed her to see and not be seen.

It was not that she had anything against her cousins. Some of them were rather lovely, and Jemima had certainly mellowed since she had married. There was her husband, there. Hugh something? Katarina stared at him. He was wearing his military uniform as usual, even though she had thought he had left the army. She would have to ask Jemima about it.

It was just—well, if Katarina could be anywhere, it would not be here, wearing her best gown, which was far too tight at the back, with earbobs that felt heavy in her ears. This gown really needed to be passed down to Maria, she thought as she twisted uncomfortably. That was the trouble with big old houses like Chalcroft. Everyone had to suffer so they could afford to heat it.

What she wouldn't give for living in a smaller but warmer home.

Katarina knew better than to say this aloud, of course. There was no possibility of the Fitzroys leaving Chalcroft. It simply could not be comprehended—and she knew her sister Olivia would rather die than not marry well enough to live in a manor just as large, just as gloomy, with so many rooms left unheated— for who could afford the coals?

"Careful!"

A cry went up, and Katarina, despite herself, peered over the banister again. The cry hadn't sounded too serious, and after a loud thunk, there were giggles echoing around the great hall.

Katarina sighed. It was only a trunk which had burst, allowing presents wrapped in brown paper to spill on the floor. It was too much to hope that it might actually be something exciting.

Lucy, one of her more mischievous cousins, had grabbed at one and was dancing around the gaggle in circles, teasing her older sister.

"Mercy, save us from raining presents!"

"Don't read those!" Jemima tried to catch Lucy as she danced past her, reading all the labels which were attached to the presents.

"You can't stop me!"

"Lucy Fitzroy, put that down or I shall cut off all your labels and—"

"Is there one for me?" Joy, the elder of the two Fitzroy cousins who lived in Bath, grinned sardonically. "Careful, Uncle William's rug!"

It all seemed so…so dull. Katarina was not one to complain, at least not out loud, but surely, she could not be the only one to think so?

Another Christmas. Another *Chalcroft* Christmas. They happened every year for her, though her cousins did not always attend in such large numbers.

The same carols would be sung around the pianoforte that Isabella would play very ill, though perhaps now Harmony was here, she could take up that particular burden. Wreath making, something she did not hate exactly but had done so many times already.

They would drink mulled wine on Christmas Eve and open presents on Christmas Day, then trot through the same old tired habits they always did.

Usually, Katarina would be the first to welcome visitors—she certainly enjoyed the distraction from the monotony of life at Chalcroft. Never going anywhere, never doing anything, never seeing anyone…

But today, Katarina simply could not muster up the enthusiasm.

A giggle. Looking sharply to her left, Katarina saw her older sister, Olivia, watching the festivities below with a smile on her face.

There was another shriek below, and then more laughter.

"What is going on," Katarina could not help but wonder aloud.

"Everyone's here!" Olivia said. Katarina jumped; clearly her sister believed she had been speaking to her. "At least, almost everyone. Caroline is giving birth apparently. Sophia stayed at home, her mother thought her too young this year, and I haven't seen Maria anywhere, have you?"

Katarina shrugged. "What does it matter to me? The same old people, the same old traditions."

As soon as the words were out of her mouth, she realized she should not have been so open. Olivia was all very well, as sisters went, and most of the time Katarina liked her. At least, there was nothing to dislike.

But Olivia treated Chalcroft with the reverence of a saint, and family to her was the greatest joy that the old place could hold.

The idea of offending Chalcroft…well, it was unthinkable.

Her sister's mouth was open. "Same old people—Kitty, they are our cousins! And you love the Chalcroft Christmas traditions!"

Katarina shrugged, for want of something better to say. It just seemed so…so dull. They had done it all before, knew the routine, and that left her bored to tears. There was so much in the world they had never explored, so much that had been hidden from them. Katarina could not recall having a conversation with someone new in months. Years, perhaps.

She was out, as much as one could be out in Society when one's father could not afford to travel to London for the Season unless he stayed with his brother, Arthur. There he was, downstairs, telling everyone that he could that Caroline would be giving birth at any minute.

And so, she just kept going around and around the year, nothing changing.

The farm on Chalcroft was the only thing worth looking at. Katarina had found herself meandering there more often lately, even in the colder winter months. At least things happened there. At least anything happened.

"Are you feeling quite well?" Olivia asked quietly. "It is not like you to—"

"It's just all so dull," Katarina let out, unable to hold it in any longer. "I mean, when one has made a single Christmas wreath, has not one made them all?"

Olivia's mouth dropped open again, but she closed it when she saw Katarina's glare.

She almost laughed at that. That was one of the benefits of sisters, she supposed. Sometimes one could communicate things without needing to say anything. Olivia was the eldest sister and so probably knew Katarina the best.

If only she did not encourage her to get into the spirit of the thing. She had had enough of that from their mother this morning.

She just…wanted to escape. Explore. See some of the world. Was that really so strange?

"You don't have to go down," Olivia said gently. "If you do not wish to."

Katarina rolled her eyes. It was so typical of Olivia. "Don't try to be like Mama, all noble. I know my due, I know I must greet everyone. But still. Gowns and jewels and opera. It's all so dull."

Olivia did not need to voice her disagreement; Katarina could see it painted across her face. That was the thing, wasn't it? Olivia loved all those things and was grateful for any chance to receive them.

"Well, I am going to go down," said Olivia, rising to her feet. "It is only polite to—"

"Olivia! Is that you—you look marvelous!"

Katarina sighed. Of course she did. Olivia always did. She was the most careful with her apparel, the most delicate with her jewels—Katarina could not recall the last time that Olivia descended the staircase without looking marvelous.

And she wasn't jealous. Not exactly.

It was more…Katarina had never been able to put it into words. Olivia already had the life she wanted. She was precisely where she wanted to be, something that Katarina craved. It wasn't that she thought her life better than most, though Katarina had to admit it probably was. They were fortunate to live in Chalcroft, fortunate to be ladies.

But Olivia's life was precisely how she wished it to be. She would make no changes. Katarina could not imagine that. She wanted…something different.

Slipping away as Olivia stepped down into the great hall, hailing her cousins, Katarina walked quietly along the corridor toward the servants' staircase.

They should really stop calling it that. The Fitzroy sisters used it just as often as the servants did. Anything to escape what their mother expected of them for that particular day.

Katarina halted her steps down the tightly wound staircase and leaned against the cold stone. It cooled her, calmed her when nothing else did.

She was full-grown, and still had to wait around at home to do whatever their mother said. Leonora was a wonderful woman, and Katarina loved her—but by her age, her mother had already married, left her country, explored, traveled, had a child!

And Katarina was still getting chastised at dinners if her hair was not perfectly curled, as Olivia's so often was.

Katarina felt the cooling stone against her back, and some of her irritation started to calm.

It was not as though she had any other choice, was it? Ladies of her social standing waited for someone to propose matrimony, preferably a duke or a viscount, she thought dryly, then one accepted.

Then you went and became a lady in another manor, with another small circle of acquaintances, with the same drafts and money worries, and different Christmas traditions. It was all so boring.

But what else was there?

"You are hiding."

Katarina stood up hastily, afraid she had been caught avoiding the crush of Fitzroys who were welcoming each other in the great hall—but when she caught sight of the speaker, she relaxed instantly and slid down the wall to sit on the steps.

"So are you," she said cheerfully to Maria.

The youngest Chalcroft Fitzroy crept up the stairs, stepped over her sister, and sat herself down on the step above her. "Maybe."

Katarina grinned. Perhaps it was always the way with four sisters; the two eldest naturally were more alike, and the younger two were more alike.

Maria was but a year or so younger than her and had the same reticence for the pageantry and nonsense that the rest of the

Fitzroy family seemed to adore—although it expressed itself in different ways.

Katarina grew irritated with everything and everyone around her, and Maria fell silent and tried to hide.

It amounted really to the same thing. Here they were, seated on the steps of the servants' staircase, hiding from their family. Olivia and Isabella were likely in the thick of it, receiving their guests, receiving the approbation of their parents.

While she and Maria…

"You did not wish to greet everyone either?"

Maria shook her head. "I do not mind seeing them later, when all of the fuss has died down, but when everyone first arrives…all those hugs and kisses, all that noise. I don't like it."

Maria was not looking at Katarina as she spoke, but it did not offend her. That was just Maria's way. When she felt comfortable, she would.

"I just think it all such a chore," Katarina admitted with a sigh and just a tad of guilt. "I mean, it's our family. We see them all the time, I do not know why there needs to be such a song and dance about it."

"That is the way we are," said Maria with a rueful smile. "The way the Fitzroys are, and Mama is no better. And I love them all, really."

"So do I," said Katarina hastily.

The last thing she needed was for anyone to believe she did not appreciate her family, because she did. Being a Fitzroy meant something, though Katarina could not easily put it into words.

Something about family, loyalty, affection, all mingled into a determination to stand by a Fitzroy no matter what. Her father and his two brothers had protected each other through thick and thin, she had always been told that, and their daughters had been raised to do the same.

Still. That did not make the same old Christmas festivities any more exciting.

"Have you heard the news?"

Katarina sighed, staring at the wall opposite. There could not be anything truly exciting. It would be something small, something their mother was excited about, no doubt, and they would all have to pretend that they were thrilled about it.

"No," she said. "One of the barn cats had kittens again? Or are we to make wreaths with different colored ribbons than last year?"

Maria snorted. "You are too sarcastic, Kitty."

It was not the sort of chastening Katarina expected, and she colored slightly to hear the mockery in her sister's voice. If Maria believed her too sarcastic, she had certainly crossed a line.

"I am sorry," she said. "It's just...do you not ever wonder what is out there, Maria?"

Maria scrunched up her nose. "Out where?"

"There," said Katarina, throwing out her hands as though that explained everything. It was obvious to her, at least.

It was quite clear that Maria was utterly at a loss. "Out there? Beyond the barns, you mean? The rest of Chalcroft Farm?"

Katarina sighed. How did one explain it? She was a lady, and that was that.

If she had been a gentleman, she would have gone up to university—to Oxford or Cambridge—and she would have traveled to London whenever she wanted in a barouche. She would have gambled, gone to art galleries, listened to concerts. She could have taken the Grand Tour, journeyed through France, seen Italy, where their mother had been born and grown. Perhaps even got as far as Greece or Turkey, seen the temples. Gone to Egypt and seen the pyramids...

But as it was, she was here. At Chalcroft. Forever, unless she married a gentleman, at which point, she would go to his manor house and sit there and wonder what color ribbon to make wreaths from. Dull, dull, dull.

"I just..." Katarina tried to put it into words for the first time. "Do you not ever wonder if there is more to life than meeting our neighbors, going to church, playing the pianoforte, and embroidery?"

"I like embroidery."

"I know you do," said Katarina with a sigh. There was no point trying to explain it to Maria. She was so set in her ways, so clear on what she enjoyed and what she did not.

It was not that Maria had no imagination; some of her embroidered creations were truly marvelous, from no pattern that Katarina had ever seen.

But when it came to something like this, something bigger, something grander…none of the Fitzroys seemed to understand it.

Katarina smiled wistfully. "Do not heed me, I speak nonsense, I am sure."

Maria blinked slowly, then shook her head. "No, I think if it matters to you, then it is probably not nonsense. You are not one to speak nonsense. Perhaps you have just not found it yet."

Found it, thought Katarina sadly. If it was there to find. It was not the sort of life that she could have, even if she found it. Ladies did not have adventures.

"We had better go upstairs," said Maria quietly. It could not be more plain that she had no desire to do so, but as the youngest, it was against her nature to disobey. "They will be expecting us in the drawing room, Kitty."

Katarina rolled her eyes and stood up. "Yes, that's precisely what they'll expect."

She started descending the steps with Maria behind her, but Katarina's mind was whirling. That was what they expected—and with so many new guests to the house, surely, she would not be missed for a few minutes?

Perhaps she could go outside, breathe in the cool air before it grew too dark. Even five minutes away from what society—and her family—expected of her would be heavenly.

"I never did tell you the news."

Katarina halted as she and her sister reached the landing, the door to the great hall before them. There was still a little murmuring on the other side of it, but it appeared that most of the Fitzroy family had moved into the drawing room as Maria had predicted. It was probably time for Katarina to stop underestimating her youngest sister. Maria may be the baby of the family, but she was no longer a baby.

"No, you didn't," said Katarina lightly. "Well?"

Maria grinned. "Papa did not tell us, but I heard one of the servants talk about it, and I looked out and saw his carriage."

Katarina frowned. "His carriage?"

There should not be anyone else arriving at Chalcroft that day—all supplies had been delivered from the village, and the London Fitzroys, always last to arrive, were already here. So, who on earth had come here?

"Luke Kingsley," said Maria, the pleasure of announcing the surprise clear on her face.

Katarina made a face. "Is that all?"

Her sister looked rather shocked. "Kitty, he is almost family! He has been coming here for years, I thought you would be pleased!"

Katarina tried to smile. "I mean, yes. Very pleased. Luke, again. How nice to have him here for Christmas."

But the truth of the matter was that Luke was just another part of the Fitzroy family, really. He had been a family friend for so long that he was an extension of them. An honorary Fitzroy.

He would likely as not throw himself into the celebrations, too, Katarina thought with a sigh. He would be more interested in wreath making than Isabella would, certainly.

Ah well. It was too much to hope that Maria's news would actually be interesting.

"Come on then." Maria's words cut across her thoughts. "We had better go into the drawing room."

And it was that moment—that moment that changed everything. Katarina looked at her sister and knew precisely what would occur if she followed her into the drawing room.

They would have polite but dull conversations with their

cousins, they would drink a little mulled wine and eat a few mince pies that Cook had baked only that morning, and they would listen to all the news from Harmony and Joy and the London Fitzroys, and they would nod and smile in all the right places…

Katarina set her jaw. Just as they had done so many times before. But not today.

"You go," she said aloud, hardly aware where all this daring had come from within her. "I am going outside."

"But—but outside? Why? You can't!" Maria said in surprise, her eyes wide. "You have to come to the drawing room and—"

"I don't have to do anything," said Katarina sharply.

"You know what I mean," Maria said reproachfully. "What shall I say if someone asks where you are?"

Katarina shrugged, taking a few steps down the servants' corridor toward the kitchens and the back door. "Say you do not know."

"But I do know!"

It was all she could do not to laugh. A rush of euphoria was pouring through Katarina's veins at the mere thought of not doing what she was told, what was expected of her. What was the point of Christmas if she was not going to have fun?

"I'll explore the stables and the barns, see what sort of carriage Luke's brought this time," said Katarina, seeing the concerned look on Maria's face. "I won't go far."

Maria frowned but made no move to follow her. "You won't get in the way of the maids milking, will you? You know how important the farm is."

Katarina smiled. "I promise."

CHAPTER TWO

I T WAS FREEZING outside. Katarina shivered as she stepped through the back door and onto the drive, the chilly December air welcoming her, tugging at her warmth. Though the sun had not yet set completely, it had dipped beneath the horizon, and only pale wan light was reaching Chalcroft now.

Light did, however, spill out from the windows where the curtains had not yet been drawn. From this side of the house, Katarina could see the drawing room. Almost everyone was in there. Only her father and Olivia, from what she could see, were missing. It was most unlike them.

Where were they?

Katarina shook her head. It was none of her concern, and she was certain if she attempted to discover their whereabouts, it would bring only chastisement that she had not been there to welcome the Fitzroy cousins in the first place.

Chalcroft's long drive stretched out before her, the stables to her left, the milking sheds just beyond them.

Katarina smiled wryly. Olivia always tried to pretend, at least to herself, that Chalcroft was some sort of ancient manor, and in a way, it was, but not in the way that she wanted.

First a farm, then a large farm, then a prosperous farm, about two hundred years ago, the Fitzroys had earned enough to build the manor house to which they aspired—but it was the large farm which gave them their wealth initially, and their father, William, had always said he would keep it running.

It gave Katarina solace, in a way, to know that though they were a gentle family, they were more interesting than that. Not just a duke in some large castle, dictating to his tenants. Not a family who could not remember from whence they gained their wealth, unable to remember what it was to work hard. Why, in the summer, the Fitzroy sisters would help with the lambing—though Olivia and Maria were not much help.

A smile crept over Katarina's lips. If all else failed, she always had the cowsheds to disappear to. Warm and soft and welcoming.

But she had not taken one step toward the sheds before a noise halted her footsteps. A carriage was rattling down the driveway at a speed most unusual for Chalcroft, as though a maniac was driving it.

Hastily taking a step back to prevent herself from being run over, Katarina watched with wide eyes as the carriage pulled to a sudden stop right before the front door.

"Dear God, man, do you want to have us killed?"

A gentleman stepped out of the carriage with a lazy grin on his face, and Katarina relaxed immediately.

"Luke!"

The man looked around and beamed. "You're not the welcoming committee I was expecting, Kitty!"

She made a face at the boy—man now, she supposed—who had visited Chalcroft so often in his youth. Tall, charming, and far too aware of it, Katarina considered Luke Kingsley to be the sort of brother she would have wanted, if she'd had a brother.

He was a complete nuisance, and she liked him.

"I think the official welcoming committee is inside," she said as Luke muttered orders to his valet, who had been clinging onto the back of the carriage for dear life, hair standing on end and completely coated in mud, as far as she could make out. "You are not expected, you know."

It was not a critique, exactly, and Katarina was pleased to see that Luke did not take it as such. That was what was so wonderful about Luke—unlike Olivia or Isabella or their mother. They always took things so seriously.

"The people who matter know I am coming," he said breezily. "You knew, of course."

Katarina grinned. "Don't try to charm me with your nonsense, that won't work."

"Ah well, you never know," said Luke with a grin. "Everyone well? Olivia, she is well?"

With a shrug, Katarina attempted to convey everything of importance. "I suppose. You are with us all Christmas, and the New Year, too?"

It would be pleasant to have someone who wasn't a Fitzroy about the place. Oh, Jemima and Harmony had wed, and their husbands were all very well, from what Katarina had seen of them. Rather doting, of course, though she supposed that couldn't be helped.

But still. Luke might be a breath of fresh air. With any luck, he could join her in refusing the old Fitzroy traditions. Perhaps do something a bit different.

"I am not sure whether you hope I am or not," said Luke with a brisk laugh. "And you know, I am not certain how long I will stay. That will depend on...on a few things."

Katarina waited for him to continue, but he did not appear to have anything more to say. The valet was pulling some luggage down from the carriage with the help of the driver, a dreadfully dressed man coated in mud from the road, and Luke glanced back at them.

"Careful with that," he said easily. "Take it around the side, I am going to meet...well, not precisely my maker."

Katarina giggled. "I would not say Papa is that intimidating."

For some reason, Luke did not answer her. In fact, he would not look at her directly in the eyes, which was rather strange. What had got into everyone today? It was most unusual for Luke to be circumspect.

"Yes," Luke said vaguely. "Well, in we go."

He offered his arm, but Katarina took an instinctive step back. "No."

"No?"

Katarina shook her head. She could not explain why, but she still had not yet had enough time on her own, away from the family. If she entered with Luke, she would have to explain to Papa and Olivia, for they were surely the welcoming committee, not only how she had known that Luke was arriving, but also where she had been going when she had met with him.

It would be criticisms and irritation, and she did not want to face that. Face her family. Find herself sucked into the dull monotony of a Chalcroft Christmas.

No, she needed a little more time than that.

"No," she said firmly. "I am going to…to do something else."

That was the marvelous thing about Luke, Katarina thought, as he shrugged and bid her goodbye. No questions, no demands, no explanations needed. He listened to what she said, nodded, and moved on.

Now why couldn't her family be more like that?

"I will see you later then, Kitty," said Luke.

Katarina opened her mouth to correct him—she was very particular about who was permitted to call her by that name. Not even her cousins were always given that right. It was special, something only her sisters and parents called her, and not always.

But just as she was about to speak, Luke opened the front door and light spilled out onto the drive.

She was standing just to the left of the door, and the driver who was doing something to the horses' tack, almost as bright as daylight.

Something twisted painfully and yet sweetly in Katarina's stomach. He was…he was the most handsome man she had ever seen.

Tall, if his height in comparison to the horses was anything to go by. Despite the mud on his boots and splattered across his livery, the formal attire was well fitted and demonstrated his strength, the broadness of his shoulders, the might of his arms.

And his face. The man had just at that moment removed his hat to brush his forehead with the back of his hand, and Katarina had a full view of his face.

It was…Katarina swallowed. Warmth was stirring in her that she had never known before. A handsome face, strong jaw, full lips, and eyes that were dark and brooding yet serious. Eyes that seemed far too intelligent for a mere driver.

Without thought, without consciously knowing what she was doing, Katarina took a step forward just as the front door closed, shutting out the light.

Yet she could still see. The driver was a few yards before her, talking softly to the horses. Katarina could just make out his words in the silence of the growing darkness.

"Well done, Bramble, good boy, Hedge," the driver was muttering, his hands patting the necks of the two horses still attached to the carriage. "Good boys…"

"Hedge?"

The man turned suddenly on his heels, all warmth from his conversation with the horses gone, and instead, a dark sort of irritable reverence replacing it.

"Yes," he said shortly. "M'lady."

Katarina took a few more steps toward him, as entranced as the horses had been. What sort of man was this? How was he having such an effect on her, an effect she did not truly understand.

All she knew was that she had to get closer to him. Close to him. She needed to hear him speak, hear more about the horses, their journey, and the driver who encouraged them onward.

Here was a man far different from the gentlemen she socialized with every day of the year. No gentleman, but a man. Not gentry, but a servant. A man who worked, who had seen the world. Who had traveled.

"The horses are named Bramble and Hedge?" Katarina asked.

There was no timidity in her voice, no hesitation. She had never been forbidden from speaking to anyone before, and besides, he was a servant, of sorts. She could speak to him as she pleased.

Yet, he did not feel like one. The driver looked down at her rather imperiously, Katarina thought, for a servant. Still, she was being a little impertinent.

"My name is Katarina Fitzroy," she said. "And you are?"

The man snorted. "So, you're one of the ladies of the house, then?"

Katarina frowned. It was not exactly an insult, but there was something in the way the man said it that made it perfectly clear that he did not believe the title recommended her.

"Bramble and Hedge," she repeated. It appeared she was not to learn the man's name, though she dearly wished to. "They are strange names."

"They are strange horses," said the man, turning away from her. "Bramblebush and Hedgerow for long, Bramble and Hedge for short."

A smile crept over Katarina's face. Well, it was rather endearing, though not as endearing as the way the man carefully caressed them. He cared about them, which was more than could be said for so many drivers Katarina had seen, on the rare occasions that they went to Bath or even London.

"They are beautiful," she said quietly.

Stepping forward without any invitation and wondering a little at her daring, she moved to the side of Hedge, who was not receiving so much attention from the driver, and patted him gently.

The horse nickered and raised his front flank but did not shy away from her.

"He likes you." The driver spoke in closely guarded wonderment.

Katarina smiled. Now the front door had been closed for a few minutes, her eyes had once again adjusted to the growing gloom. She could see the driver well now, though he carefully avoided her eyes.

And that's as it should be, Katarina tried to remind herself. She was a lady of the house, and he a mere servant. A servant of someone else, to boot.

But something about him made her hesitate, made her stay. Words would not have explained it but…There was something about him.

"Do you have a name like theirs?" she asked mischievously, her smile tugging at her lips.

The driver met her gaze, then dropped it to look at the horses. "No."

Katarina sighed. All patience disappearing, the words that she would have thought before and never would have said poured from her mouth, untamed.

"For goodness's sake, at least try to be interesting! If you do not give me sufficiently diverting conversation, I shall be forced to go inside and talk to my family!"

The man chuckled; it was a dry, sarcastic laugh, but a laugh, nonetheless. "You are not like most of the young ladies I have met, Miss Fitzroy."

Katarina made a face. "Don't call me that—that's my sister. And two of my cousins—'tis complicated. Just call me Katarina."

The man looked at her once more, and this time Katarina's breath caught in her throat. There was such an intensity in his look there—desire, perhaps, though the very thought of it made her blush in the darkness. Interest and a little intrigue.

"Isaac…Isaac Emmett," he said finally with a wry smile. "Though why a lady like you would care about talking with someone like me—"

"Nonsense," Katarina said curtly. "You know, we have an Isaac."

That did surprise him. "I was given to understand there were four Fitzroy daughters, but no sons."

Only then did Katarina realize her mistake, and she lost herself in peals of laughter for a few moments as Isaac looked on with amazement.

"Oh, no, I did not mean…" said Katarina with a grin. "Come on, let's get Bramble and Hedge to the stables."

"But—"

"No buts," said Katarina cheerfully. "Come on."

She gently encouraged the horses to step forward slowly, and Isaac had no choice but to walk with them. Katarina looked at the ground as they went, somehow unable to meet his gaze once again.

What was she doing? Helping out a driver? Surely she had better things to do than this?

Yet, there was something about him. Katarina could see it, even if she could not explain it. Something that drew her to him. Something that attracted her. Something that made it difficult to even consider going back into the house, not without spending more time with him. Getting to know him.

He was the sort of man that she would very much like to kiss.

Katarina flushed at the thought. Now where had that come from? It was ridiculous to consider such a thing!

Yet there was something so…so sensual about him. So tactile. As Isaac strode ahead to open up the stable doors, as he unharnessed the horses and rubbed them down, Katarina watched in silence. Words did not appear necessary. The driver seemed to have accepted her presence there, and Katarina respected his craft too much to interrupt him.

After half an hour or so, however, the horses were brushed down, fed, watered, and placed in their stables. Katarina had been seated on a large hay bale, a piece of hay twirling between her fingertips, and Isaac, warm, brushing a little sweat and mud from his brow, removed his jacket and rolled up his sleeves.

Katarina swallowed and attempted not to look at the strength in his arms. There was a man who could catch her if she fell. Who could carry her, probably. If he pulled her into his arms…

"So," said Isaac, washing his hands in the water butt and

jolting Katarina to her senses. "Who is this other Isaac?"

Katarina smiled weakly. It seemed so silly now, but she had to answer. "Our bull."

He laughed at that, a low, dark laugh that seemed soft at the same time. "Should I be offended that I am so compared?"

"I did not compare you," reminded Katarina, her heart thumping. Why was her heart doing such strange things inside her chest? "I merely said that you shared the same name. We have a dairy herd here, for the milk, you know, and so we need a…a bull."

Heart seared her cheeks. Well, it was not a very seemly thing to discuss at all, let alone with a stranger. Such things were…base. Scandalous.

But Isaac Emmett did not feel like a stranger. Though Katarina could not explain it, she felt just as comfortable with him as Luke, and she had known him for years. It made no sense.

As Isaac came toward her and leaned against a stall with a lazy smile on his face, something deep within Katarina lurched. She…she was attracted to him. There was no point in denying it, even if it was only to herself.

Besides, it was not as though anything could come of such a thing. A strange infatuation, that was all it would be, she told herself. Nothing permanent. He would be gone in a few days.

"Shouldn't you be inside with your family?" asked Isaac, an eyebrow raised.

Katarina swallowed. It was not like her to criticize her family, and to a stranger, even more strange. Not that she had many occasions of meeting anyone new for them to be a stranger.

But then, she did not need to criticize them. She just needed to tell the truth.

"I would rather be here with you," she said honestly.

Isaac's second eyebrow rose to meet the first. "Well, you do surprise me."

A little fire sparked in her stomach. "Why?"

The driver sighed. "Well, you should know why. 'Tis not

difficult. Here you are, the daughter of a fine family in a fine manor. I bet you've got a pianoforte and a library and all sorts of things in that house of yours."

Katarina flushed. Well, of course it did—some manor Chalcroft would be without them!

But for some reason, she felt a little flustered and did not wish to agree that the house contained such things. What for Olivia would be symbols of their class, their gentry status, were somehow…tainted.

If Isaac did not have them, Katarina found herself thinking she did not want them.

"You are a lady," said Isaac with a smile. "A real lady, not just someone who is born on the correct side of the blanket."

Now Katarina could feel the heat in her cheeks. Oh, why did they have to betray her so? "I don't know what you mean."

"Yes, you do," said Isaac. He stepped toward her, closing the gap between them. Katarina felt her heart skip a beat most uncomfortably. "You know exactly what I mean. Some ladies live in little terraced houses in London, but you? You live in a mansion. You have all you could ever want, and no one will ever take that from you. You shouldn't be seen out here with a mere driver."

He went to turn away, but he was close enough now for Katarina to touch him—and to her great surprise, she did.

Caring not for the fact that she was in one of her best gowns, chosen to honor the Fitzroy cousins, or that Isaac was coated in mud and muck and straw, she reached out and took his hand in hers.

Isaac halted, turning around in astonishment to look at her.

Katarina smiled shyly, hardly aware of what she was going to do next. What happened next? How was she supposed to know? This was all most scandalous, and he was absolutely right. Her family would have a fit if they saw her in the stables with a servant.

But Isaac Emmett was by far the most fascinating person she

had ever met, and he was handsome. And tall. And made her warm all over.

Katarina may not be a very worldly woman, but she knew enough about love and matrimony to know what it was she wanted from Isaac. Not that she would ever be able to say it, of course.

"I...you are more interesting than my family," Katarina said in a slightly constricted voice. She cleared her throat and tried again. "I would like to talk to you. To know you."

Isaac's fingers were warm and strong, entangled in hers. "Know me?"

His voice was low, and Katarina flushed at the hint of a suggestion in his words. "That...that isn't what I—"

"Isn't it?" Isaac cut across her, closing the gap between them. He was so tall as he stood beside the hay bale on which she was seated. So tall and so charming.

Katarina stared into his eyes. She could stare into them forever. What was it, pulling her to him, refusing to let her depart? And could she have it forever?

"You are interesting, too, Miss Katarina Fitzroy," said Isaac. "If you were a maid or a dairymaid of this house, perhaps I would take you at your word. I would give you a tumble in this here straw, show you precisely what you were missing. Give you pleasure you had never known before."

Katarina's breath caught in her throat, and warmth pooled between her legs as a dull ache started to creep through her bones.

The idea of Isaac Emmett even kissing her...

"And that would show you," said Isaac quietly, "that we are different, you and I. You are a lady of the house, and I am a—"

"Man of the stables," breathed Katarina, unable to look away from him, finding her mouth revealed the secrets of her heart without her consciously considering it. "And wouldn't you like to know, just for a moment, what it was to kiss a lady of the house?"

Isaac's eyes darkened. A quick movement of his hand, and

Katarina was on her feet, standing before him, pressed up against him. Only now could she feel how his heart was thumping heavily through his shirt and waistcoat, in time with hers.

Katarina did gasp this time. "Isaac, we—"

"This is what you wanted," he said, lowering his head slowly, his lips just above her own. "Remember that, Katarina Fitzroy. This is what you wanted. What you asked for. What, if I am any judge, you would beg for."

Heart quivering, Katarina allowed her eyes to close as Isaac lowered his lips to hers and—

"Katarina? Katarina, are you out here? Dinner has started!"

Katarina opened her eyes. Isaac's lips were half an inch from hers, but just as she leaned forward to capture them, he raised his head.

"It seems you are missed," he said with a wry smile. "And there will be a space at the kitchen table in the servants' hall for me. Two different tables. Two different worlds."

Katarina could not speak, the intensity of the moment almost overwhelming her.

Isaac grinned as he dropped her hand and stepped away. "Good evening, Miss Katarina Fitzroy."

CHAPTER THREE

"**B**UT YOU HAVE always loved wreath making!"

"I know," came the voice of Olivia from the library. "And I enjoyed it last year, and the year before, and countless years before that. And I do not want to do it this year."

Katarina had been walking past in almost a dream, hardly paying attention to where she was going, her mind entirely focused on what had occurred yesterday.

Yesterday. It was hard to believe it was only a day past. Less than twenty-four hours.

So much seemed to have changed in that time. So much of who she was had changed. Irrevocably.

"It seems you are missed. And there will be a space at the kitchen table in the servants' hall for me. Two different tables. Two different worlds."

Katarina seemed to be halfway between embarrassment and delight whenever she thought back to the conversation she had shared with Isaac Emmett, driver to Luke Kingsley, and the tantalizing kiss that had never quite happened.

At least, it had not happened in reality. In her imagination, of course, it had happened several times, each time slightly different.

Sometimes soft. Sometimes hard. Sometimes it was reverential, Isaac's hands staying with hers. Other times, his hands moved to her waist, her buttocks, pulling her closer…

None of them, she was sure, would ever live up to the reality of what a kiss from Isaac would have been like. Scalding. Intense. Wonderful.

Katarina was certain, somehow, though she could not understand why, that whatever kiss Isaac would have bestowed on her in that moment would have been far beyond her understanding.

"But you love wreath making!" Harmony's voice echoed from the open door of the library. "You love it!"

Katarina sighed. The annual wreath making. Her cousin was not wrong, Olivia was usually the first to start making a wreath, eager to correct all the others on precisely how it was supposed to be done.

There was nothing her older sister Olivia liked more than telling others what to do.

Yet for some reason, some of Katarina's own malaise appeared to have spread to her elder sister. Despite her excitement yesterday at the arrival of all the family, the beginning of the Christmas season proper, Olivia had looked rather unwell at dinner last night and sounded even worse now.

Katarina lingered outside the library for a moment, intrigued to hear what was going on.

"What's happening now?"

Katarina flushed, but Joy did not seem to care that she had caught one of her cousins eavesdropping.

"Olivia is making a fuss, as usual," Katarina said quietly.

Joy grinned. "Marvelous. I could do with some entertainment."

"I said, I do not wish to make wreaths," came Olivia's voice from the library.

Joy raised her eyebrows mockingly, and Katarina giggled as her cousin entered the room, leaving her outside.

"What's all this fuss?"

"Olivia—*Olivia*—says that she will not be partaking in wreath making this year!" came Harmony's reply from inside the room.

Katarina could not help but grin. Joy was a little sharp sometimes, a little too cutting with her tongue, but she liked her. It was nice to have someone else in the house who saw the gentle ways to tease others around them.

"Nonsense," came Joy's cheerful voice. "I am sure she merely wishes to give us visitors enough time to play with it all ourselves before she sweeps in and makes improvements."

Katarina snorted, then covered her mouth with her hands. She was not entirely sure what Olivia would say if she knew her younger sister had been listening outside the room, but it was surely not something pleasant.

"What on earth are you doing out here?"

Katarina whirled around, her shoulders taut and her heart racing, convinced she had been caught, before she smiled at the sight of Luke Kingsley striding toward her.

"You gave me such a fright!" she said severely, waggling her finger at him. "How dare you creep up on me!"

Luke grinned. "Listening at the door?"

"They are having such a nonsensical conversation, I dare not enter for fear of becoming dull myself," Katarina said, rolling her eyes. "But then I have nowhere else to go."

"There's wreath making in the gun room," said Luke.

She could not help but laugh at that. "You are a true Fitzroy, Luke, if you believe that to be the pinnacle of the day!"

Luke sighed. "Yes, I suppose you are right. Still, it could be a rather useful means to an end, if I time this properly. If I am clever about it."

Katarina frowned. Means to an end? She had no idea what he meant by that, but then, Luke had been rather strange since he had arrived a few days ago. She had thought, when her father had announced that they would be hosting a Christmas Eve ball, with several neighbors invited, that Luke would be a little more pleased. But for some reason, the idea of more gentlemen arriving to thin out the number of ladies at Chalcroft this Christmas seemed to have disappointed him. Most strange.

There was no sense of disappointment on Luke's face in this

moment, however. On the contrary, he was looking at the library door with a glint in his eyes.

And she knew that look.

"Luke Kingsley," said Katarina quietly. "What are you up to?"

"Me? Up to?" Luke grinned. "Can't imagine what you mean, Kitty. Will you be wreath making?"

Katarina made a face, and this time it did not even occur to her to correct her name. "Not unless you drag me, kicking and screaming."

He barked a laugh at that. "I don't imagine many ladies are like you, Kitty. Well, wish me luck. Come on you three, are you not going to the gun room for wreath making?"

Luke spoke the last sentence as he entered the library, to general great surprise, from what Katarina could hear through the door.

What on earth did he mean?

"I don't imagine many ladies are like you, Kitty."

Katarina frowned as she meandered away from the library, certain Luke would be persuading Olivia to join him in wreath making, and not wishing to be seen lingering by the door—or dragged along to the gun room to make silly Christmas wreaths.

Perhaps she was not like so many ladies. Slipping into the drawing room, which had such a beautiful view of the drive, Katarina thought back to that moment when she had first seen Isaac.

Isaac Emmett. She had been unable to rid her mind of thoughts of Isaac from the moment she had been interrupted in her tantalizing first kiss—or what should have been her first kiss—and forced to dine with her respectable family. Respectable, dull family.

There was something about him. Something about the way he was so different, so…so uncouth and yet refined. Isaac did not say things to impress, as Luke often did, Katarina was sure. He spoke from the heart. From the gut.

It was mesmerizing.

"You appear a little warm, Olivia." It was Luke's voice; he had evidently encouraged Olivia to leave the library and go to the gun room to make wreaths, though in Katarina's view, her sister sounded a little harassed as their footsteps passed the drawing room.

"Nonsense," came the flustered and unconvincing response from Olivia.

Katarina waited a moment until their footsteps had disappeared down the corridor, then sighed heavily. The entire family—or at least, most of them—would be in the gun room, getting holly and ivy everywhere.

And that meant…

The thought occurred to her so quickly, Katarina was only just able to grasp at it as it fluttered through her mind. If all the Fitzroys were wreath making, that meant she could slip out of the house, and do…something else.

She was not looking for Isaac, she told herself firmly as she stepped into the corridor and pulled on a riding habit of Isabella's which had been abandoned by the front door. She was just going outside. Fresh air was very good for one's health, after all.

Katarina grinned as she opened the door. Well. She was not able to completely convince herself.

Breathing in sharply as the cold air hit her face, she shivered but stepped out boldly into the bright but chilly sunlight. There was nothing quite like Chalcroft in December, even Katarina had to admit it—not that she would do so in Olivia's hearing.

The manor house was pretty against the blue of the sky, and there was a sense of movement and busyness just past the stables. Katarina meandered over there, hands in the pockets of her riding habit to keep them warm, and smiled as she saw the milkmaids bringing in the cows.

"Careful there, Molly!" she called out as one cow mischievously attempted to avoid the milking shed.

Molly grinned back. "Hello there, Miss Katarina! Going to give us a hand today?"

Katarina looked ruefully down at her gown and riding habit. Both were of the finest silks, and the riding habit wasn't even hers. At least, it would be, but for now it was Isabella's.

"I cannot help I am afraid," she said sadly. "But I'll join you, keep you company."

There was much ruckus in the cowshed. The eight dairy heifers which had been brought in were each attended by a milkmaid. Katarina knew them all by name, cows and girls. They were just as much a part of Chalcroft as she and her sisters were. Perhaps more so, as it was on their milk and their calves that the farm depended.

Settling herself comfortably on a hay bale as was her custom, Katarina made sure to stay out of the way of the girls as they moved around the cowshed, gently encouraging one cow forward at a time to be milked.

There was something rather soothing about it all. The world could get itself tangled in knots, Olivia could make a great show of not wanting to make a wreath, and then suddenly find herself persuaded by Luke, which made no sense, the whole Fitzroy family could descend—but cows were cows.

No matter what happened in the world, rain or shine, warm or cold, whether or not Isabella had a spot on her nose or Maria could be found, the cows needed milking, and the milkmaids would do their work.

Sometimes she envied them. Oh, not the muck and the exhaustion, Katarina was not so foolish as to fail to see beyond her rose-tinted view of the country ways.

But still. Molly and the other seven milkmaids, they had a purpose in life. They knew precisely where they should be at all times, and what they should be doing. At the end of a long day, they at least had the satisfaction of knowing they had performed a job well done.

And what did she have? Another boring recital of Isabella's to applaud, or a piece of Maria's embroidery to look at?

Even when the Fitzroy cousins arrived, it was to coo over the news of Caroline's new baby, or marvel at the way Harmony played the pianoforte.

Dull, dull, dull.

"Now what is a lady like you doing here?"

Katarina rose to her feet immediately, startled into the sudden movement by the recognition of the man's voice.

Isaac's voice. He was standing just behind the hay bale, a wry smile on his face and his hands in his pockets. There was a piece of straw in his mouth, and he was dressed not in the muddy road clothes of a driver, but in the livery of the Kingsley colors.

Katarina tried to smile. All she had to do was act like a normal human being, she told herself silently, wishing that her heart was not thumping quite so loudly. How difficult could that be?

Isaac grinned. "Caught in the act, I see."

Katarina raised herself up as best she could. "Not at all. The cowsheds are not forbidden, and I come here often to help."

"Help?" Isaac raised an eyebrow. "I can see that. Very helpful, the way you watch those milkmaids do all the hard work."

She had to smile ruefully. "Well, I am usually more help in the spring, if I am honest. I had not intended to come down here this morning, or I would have worn a cotton gown."

If only she had not mentioned what she was wearing. Before Katarina could say another word, Isaac's gaze was drifting down her, taking in her riding habit.

Why was it that his eyes seemed to…well. Linger. Linger on certain parts of her body. Katarina could not help but feel a little flush at the intensity of his expression. Did he admire what he saw, perhaps? Or was it all much the same to him, just another lady in a fancy gown?

And what did it matter?

"And what about you?" Katarina said, more to distract herself from the strange thoughts flitting through her mind. "Are you helping?"

Isaac leaned against the hay bale. "No, I am not."

She waited for him to continue, but he did not appear to be.

"You are…you are dressed as a footman today."

He grinned. "That I am."

He really was most infuriating, Katarina thought. The least he could do was be a better conversationalist! Why was he leaving her to do all the hard work? It was most irritating.

"Well?" she said a little sharply. "Is that all you can say for yourself?"

Isaac shrugged. "What else is there to say?"

"You could make more of an effort," Katarina said.

His dark eyes met hers with such force that she almost took a step backward. It was a look most unusual in a servant—as though he were a prince gazing down at her, one of his subjects. As though she had been impertinent, not him, and she should apologize to him directly.

Katarina was in half a mind to do so, merely to end the look. How did a man like that stare at her so? How did a servant know how to be so imperious? Did he not…well. Did he not like her?

"You forget yourself, Miss Katarina," said Isaac slowly. "You are a lady, and I am a servant. I am bid to obey my lord, and not you."

With that, he turned away from her and started toward the door of the cowshed.

Katarina's mouth fell open. To speak to her in such a way… It was outrageous!

Yet merited, a small voice in the back of her mind reminded her. What is he to you? Just a servant who happens to be staying in Chalcroft for the festive season. Once it is all over, and Luke disappears as he always does, he will take his servants with him. Isaac will disappear, and you won't see him again until Luke returns. Whenever that will be. If he brings Isaac at all.

Katarina swallowed. She could not think of that now, could not think of Isaac's imminent departure. The idea that she had offended him pained her. She had never felt this way about another servant before, though of course, she had never spoken so rashly to a servant before. It was not in her nature.

Something about Isaac Emmett riled her.

"Wait!" Katarina rushed forward and reached Isaac just as he left the cowshed. The cold air made her shiver, but she spoke on regardless. She owed him that. "I…I am sorry."

Isaac raised an eyebrow as she fell in step beside him as he walked through the farmyard toward the stables. "And why would you say a thing like that?"

"Because I spoke rudely to you, and I am sorry for it."

He suddenly halted, right outside the stable. Katarina stared at him, lungs tight at the effort of keeping up with his long legs, and looked up into his eyes.

There was an impenetrable expression on them. Desire, yes, she could see that now. She had only seen it a few times in the eyes of foolish young men that her father had invited over for dancing practice, and it had repulsed her then.

It did not repulse her now. Quite the opposite. Isaac stared down at her, so masculine in the way he looked and stood that Katarina shivered.

She wanted him to kiss her. He never would, of course. That would be most irregular—and she could hardly ask for such a thing. It had been a strange set of circumstances before, one that, surely, she would be unable to repeat.

Still. She wanted it.

"You are sorry for it," Isaac repeated.

Katarina nodded. She could still hear the lowing of the cows in the cowshed, and the gentle chatter of the milkmaids, but other than that, they were alone.

She and Isaac were alone.

"You do not even know what you are apologizing for," Isaac said, taking a step toward her. Katarina stepped back hastily, her back meeting the stable door. "Look at you, in your beautiful gown, and your beautiful hair, you have no comprehension of what a hard day's labor is, do you?"

Katarina swallowed, her eyes wide. "You…you think my hair is beautiful?"

Isaac swore under his breath and grinned wryly. "Is that all you heard?"

"No, I heard it all," said Katarina breathlessly. Why was it so difficult to breathe at the moment? Why did Isaac's gaze seem to take the air from her lungs? "But you're wrong. At least, you're right, but you are also wrong. I know what it is to work hard—you should see us here in the spring. We may be Fitzroys, but we're not—not noble, or anything! We all work hard in the spring and summer on the farm, and just because I am dressed like this, that doesn't mean I don't know the sweat on my brow, or the relief when a calf is born, or-or the desire to…"

Katarina's voice trailed away as heat seared her cheeks. That was close. She had very nearly said something that was most unbecoming of a lady. Certainly something she should not even be thinking.

Isaac took a step closer to her, and Katarina attempted to retreat before remembering she had her back to the stable wall. She was trapped between the upright wood and the strength of Isaac's chest, and she found to her horror and delight that there was nowhere else she would rather be.

"Desire," repeated Isaac in a low voice, his gaze flickering to her lips, then back to her eyes. "What would you know about desire?"

Katarina swallowed. "I…I know it now."

There was a moment, a split second when nothing happened, nothing moved, and Katarina knew to her eternal shame that she had gone too far. What had possessed her to say such a thing! Out loud, of all things, and to a man like Isaac. A man she barely knew, yet a man who seemed to know her perfectly.

And then in a rush of desire and heat and fury, Isaac pushed her shoulders against the wall, crushing her with his chest, as he took her head in his hands and kissed her furiously, as though a lifetime of passion had been pent up within him and had finally broken free.

Katarina shivered in his hands, felt the pressure of his lips, was certain that she would resist, for a Fitzroy should not be accepting kisses from anyone, let alone a servant!

But she did not. She melted, pleasure flowing through her as Isaac's kiss, both devilishly passionate yet tender, made her quiver with unexpected sensuality.

His hands were soft, determined to entrap her, yet brought such tingles across her neck that Katarina was glad she was leaning against the stables, else her feet would not support her.

The kiss deepened. Isaac's tongue teased across her lips, and Katarina's fingers clutched at his lapels as she permitted him entrance, moaning slightly as the pleasure deepened.

Dear God, if this was one kiss, she could not understand why people did not do this continuously. Her head spun, her world changed forever in that moment, and Isaac's furious passion did not cease.

"Katarina Fitzroy, what are you doing to me," he groaned as he pulled away from her, but she tugged at his lapels to bring him closer, to kiss her again.

All she wanted was for Isaac Emmett to kiss her every day of her life.

After a few minutes, Katarina could not tell how many, Isaac broke the kiss and let his hand hang beside hers.

"Dear God," he whispered. "I was not expecting that."

Katarina clung to him, hardly enough strength in her to stand. "Neither was I."

Isaac's eyes met hers as he lifted his head. "I did not offend— you did not—"

She did not want to hear such words, wanted him to forget all thoughts of not kissing her again. Ignoring her own better judgment and the whispers of her heart that this would never last, that kissing a coachman in the stable yard while her family were inside the house was something she would surely regret later, Katarina pulled Isaac closer.

"Do not speak," she whispered. "Just kiss me."

CHAPTER FOUR

"**A**ND WE MUST have more candles—*more* candles, I say, not fewer!" Leonora Fitzroy, Katarina's mother, was on the warpath, and her daughters were doing precisely what they did whenever this occurred: hiding.

"I do not want to hear excuses, they sell candles in town, procure them no matter the cost!" their mother was saying as she marched down a corridor.

Katarina had heard her coming a mile off, of course. It was always the way at Chalcroft; something about the corridors made it immensely easy to hear the echoes of what was before and behind you.

When it was one's mother ranting about candles, the best thing to do was hide. She had slipped into the library, only to see with a smile that Isabella and two of their cousins, Esther and Harmony, had already had the same idea.

"Do you think she'll come in here?" asked Esther anxiously. "Not that I would wish to avoid your mother, of course," she added hastily.

Katarina snorted. "Do not fear, we are all equally concerned about running into Mama when she is in this sort of mood. What Papa thought, announcing a ball with less than a week's notice..."

"You had the same a few years ago," Harmony nodded sagely from the fireplace, where she had previously been immersed in a book. "Caroline's engagement ball, do you remember telling me, Esther?"

"I do indeed," said Esther, returning her gaze to the shelves, where she appeared to be hunting down a particular book. "So much ruckus that year, I thought Christmas would have to be cancelled so we did not all fall down with exhaustion."

"Wasn't that the year Jemima became engaged, too?" Isabella asked. She was seated in the window box, a collection of books scattered around her, but none seeming of interest.

Katarina walked over to the seat beside her. There was something so dependable about her sister Isabella. Olivia was prone to "fits of feelings," as their father called it, and Maria could usually not be discovered unless absolutely necessary, often hiding away from her own family.

But Isabella was usually calm. She appeared bored in this moment, of course, but that was beside the point. Katarina knew that feeling well.

Seating herself, she allowed the chatter between her sister and her cousins to wash over her.

"—and a solider to boot, we never thought it would—"

"Well, a drummer really, is it the same thing?"

"I think him mightily handsome." This was Esther, of course. Katarina hid a smile as she looked at her cousin who had a dreamy expression. "Not as handsome as Caroline's husband, of course."

"Well, he is the Earl of Cheshire," said Isabella with a laugh. "It is amazing how a gentleman's features are greatly improved by such a title!"

Laughter rang out in the library, quickly hushed to ensure Leonora did not find them.

Katarina smiled wistfully. A title. Yes, it was all very well to have a title. When she had been young—at least younger than she was now—she had often wondered who she and her sister and cousins would end up marrying.

So far, only three of them had married. Jemima had married a solider, Harmony a musician—no surprises there—and Caroline had married her sweetheart.

The fact that Stuart was a hardworking doctor with no wealth to his name had not mattered to the Fitzroy family—and it certainly had not mattered when it emerged, quite to their shared surprise, that he was the heir to an earldom.

Yet that sort of thing had never truly appealed to Katarina. It was only now she thought about it, with the gentle chatter of her sister and cousins around her, that Katarina realized just how different her expectations of love and matrimony were.

They spoke of love, yes, but also of prestige, of title, of wealth. Of where they would live, what they would do, who they would know. All the trappings of a marriage, not the man himself.

When she had spent a little time thinking of the sort of gentleman she wished to marry, she realized with crimson cheeks, that he was not even necessarily a gentleman.

"Katarina Fitzroy, what are you doing to me?"

The heat searing Katarina's cheeks blossomed into pink, she was sure. She had been wild, a little too wild, to permit that—yet she had no regrets.

The way Isaac kissed her…it made Katarina feel alive in a way she had never felt before. As if she had been asleep for the last twenty years and had never known what it felt to truly be awake.

He woke something in her that had been dormant. Or maybe it had never been there before. Maybe Isaac had not stirred something with her, exactly, but poured something within her as his lips had poured down passion, he had sparked something new inside her.

Katarina shivered, despite the warmth of the room. It was most unlike her to do anything like that. Her first kiss, and with a servant against a stable wall, for goodness's sake!

She would not have it any other way.

She smiled to herself, watching Esther and Harmony fight comfortably about how many dances they would dance at tomorrow's Christmas Eve ball.

"You surely do not think you can dance them all!"

"Why on earth not? I have more than enough energy, and if Uncle William is correct, and several gentlemen will be attending—"

"We cannot have all nine of us ladies dancing at the same time!"

Katarina smiled lazily. It all seemed so strange now, so distant. If Luke had not arrived, had not decided to spend Christmas here with them all—a decision that she still did not really understand, when, surely, he had his own home that he could invite friends to—then Isaac would not have come here.

And she would not have known the joy of that kiss. Of Isaac. Of realizing that there was something about him, beyond herself, that she desperately wanted to know.

She had gone out that morning, early, before any of the other Fitzroy were awake. Heart in her mouth, Katarina knew that if she was glimpsed from the house, disappearing into the stables, there would be some rather awkward questions for her by the time she returned for breakfast.

It did not matter, anyway. Isaac was not there. She had not been able to find him.

Katarina had sat most irritably on the hay bale for several minutes before she realized that Isaac must be breakfasting with the rest of the servants. Though the temptation to creep down there and see if she could have a word with him rose in her heart, Katarina most sensibly forced it down.

It would be difficult enough to explain to her family why she had gone into the stables so early that morning. It would have been nigh on impossible to find a justification for bothering a servant—a male servant, and belonging to a different family, to boot!—while he broke his fast.

And so, Katarina had not seen him.

For some reason, it pained her to be without him. Katarina had never known anything like it—a dull ache in her stomach, as though she had not eaten in days.

Being apart from him, this strange servant who looked at her with the same imperiousness of a sultan, yet was a mere driver, was painful. She needed to be with him. Being apart from him was no longer acceptable.

Where it would lead, Katarina could not tell—but the idea of not seeing him today was eating her up inside, making it impossible to concentrate on anything.

This was proven when she received a gentle shove in the shoulder.

"Kitty!"

"Wh-What?" stammered Katarina, looking up.

Isabella was smiling but with a frown on her face. "You haven't heard a word I was saying, have you?"

Katarina smiled weakly. There was no point in lying. If there was one thing Fitzroy sisters did not do to each other, it was lie.

Unless greatly provoked, of course. She could think of no reason why she would ever tell anyone of that kiss—that head-spinning kiss.

"No," she admitted. "Please, tell me again."

It was not that she had much interest in what Isabella was saying, whatever it was, but Katarina had to hope that the topic would at least keep her amused for a little while.

As it was, it was another set of dull speculation—this time, to her slight surprise about Olivia. Olivia and Luke. Olivia and Luke?

"I just think something strange is going on there," said Isabella thoughtfully, opening and closing the book in her lap without giving it much attention. "Do not you think?"

Katarina frowned. "Olivia—and Luke? Luke is…well. *Luke.*"

Isabella shrugged. "I am not saying that I understand it—quite the opposite, I am at a total loss to understand what I see, but I am seeing something. The way they look at each other—did you notice, when we made wreaths?"

Katarina smiled, unable to help herself. So, her absence had not been missed, then. That was a small mercy.

"I did not spot it, no," she said smoothly. Well, it was not a lie. Not really. She had not said anything that was untrue. "What precisely have you seen?"

"Well, I do not know that it is something one can put into words," Isabella said thoughtfully.

Katarina watched Esther and Harmony continue to bicker quite happily about what gowns they would wear to the ball. The Christmas Eve ball. Perhaps another year she may have been excited about it, perhaps even joined in their conversation, discussed whether to swap sashes or ribbons to make her tired old gown look a little more interesting.

But it was a ball, and that meant gentry. Isaac Emmett would not be receiving an invitation to attend; she doubted her father even knew his name, yet the man was staying here in his house.

No, the ball would be nothing if it did not contain Isaac, and as it did not...

"I just think they are too...friendly."

Katarina looked up. Isabella was doing something complicated with her fingers, entangling them in a strange way, as though that explained everything perfectly.

"Friendly?" she repeated.

"You know what I mean," said Isabella expressively. Katarina was reminded irresistibly of their mother. "Whenever one of them is looking at the other, they have this strange look on their faces, like the whole world is...softer. And as soon as the other one looks up, the first looks away!"

Katarina thought about it. She had not noticed Luke being any different than normal, and Olivia's emotions were always so wild, it was difficult to know when she was being different, or just...Olivia.

"I don't know," she said slowly. "What you're talking about sounds like—"

"Love," sighed Isabella happily. "I know."

Katarina snorted. "You cannot be serious! Luke and Olivia! Issy, we have known him almost our entire lives!"

"But he is not our brother, not really," countered Isabella, lowering her voice. Katarina glanced around, but it did not appear that Esther nor Harmony had heard them. "And love, Kitty, love is such a precious thing. For love to be requited like that, between two people who know each other so well, have known each other for years—is that not wonderful?"

Katarina swallowed. It was wonderful in a way. Olivia was the eldest Fitzroy, and she had a not insignificant dowry, like all of them, but she was not in Society much, and their dowries and name alone would not be sufficient to attract a good match— certainly not nobility.

And Luke was a lord. Lord Kingsley. That would make Olivia a lady, if they married.

But still…there was something so strange about the idea of looking up at someone you knew well, a person you had spent years with, and suddenly seeing them in a completely different light—after all, they had all swam in the river together as children, stripped off in the village pond, dipped in the fountain!

Katarina flushed at the very thought of it. It was unconscionable that they had done it, in hindsight. Luke was a gentleman!

But as children, it had not mattered. She had never seen Luke as a man, not really. He was just one of the family.

But if Olivia cared for him, then obviously something had changed for her. What was that like, Katarina wondered. For someone to transform before your eyes into someone you considered a brother, and then suddenly someone you would…

Well. She felt her stomach swoop. Someone you wished to kiss against a stable wall.

Surely Olivia had no wish to do that with Luke…did she?

"I do not know," Katarina said slowly. "It still feels a little strange."

Isabella shrugged. She had opened up her book now and was clearly done with the conversation that she herself had started.

"I don't know," she said. "Luke is handsome enough, I suppose, and is well-born. He has a title. He is wealthy, I think, though of course I have never asked. He is the perfect sort of match for a Fitzroy."

"The perfect sort of match for a Fitzroy."

Katarina swallowed. She had never said the words aloud before, but now Isabella had done so, she was right.

There was a certain kind of man that their father would wish to hear requests of marriage from, and it was someone like Luke. Someone confident and cocky, who knew the family, who came from the right sort of family himself.

Someone with money and land and a title. It was everything her father would want. But was it what she wanted?

"But Jemima and Harmony did not marry wealthy men, nor men with titles," Katarina said quietly. "They married a soldier and a penniless musician."

Isabella laughed gently under the continued ball chatter by the fireplace. "Yes, but they are...well, they are not *Chalcroft* Fitzroys, are they? Our father is the eldest of his three brothers. We are the ones who live at the seat of the family—you really think our father would allow us to wed just anyone?"

Katarina blinked. It had never occurred to her before. She had always wanted to be happy, nothing more. Money and titles would make Olivia happy, probably; she always did like a little more luxury than Chalcroft could offer.

But to give that all up, all the luxury and finery of a good match, for happiness? Katarina would do it in a heartbeat.

"So..." Katarina swallowed. She knew this was a foolish thing to ask, but there was no one else in the family to whom she could posit this question. Olivia would immediately suppose something terrible, and Maria would merely flush and say nothing. And the idea of asking her mother...

Isabella looked up from her book. "Did you say something?"

Katarina cleared her throat. She would ask the question; she was not a coward. "So do you think if I had...if I had made the acquaintance of a gentleman...more of a man, really...who had neither wealth, nor name, nor title, that Papa would not permit the match?"

Isabella burst into peals of laughter. "Oh, Kitty, you do make me laugh! What on earth are you talking about, meeting someone without money or title or…"

Her voice trailed away as Katarina looked her straight in the face, without a smile nor a frown. It took all her self-control, but she did not look away.

The horror on Isabella's face told her she had finally taken in her words.

"But…but you cannot be serious," said Isabella in a low voice, her expression stricken. "Truly, you have met someone with whom you have fallen in love? You have decided on him, that he will make you happy, even if he breaks our father's heart?"

"That is not what I said," Katarina said hastily.

It did not seem to matter. "But why bring it up at all, if it had not occurred?" said Isabella urgently, closing her book on her finger and looking seriously at her sister. "Who is it? Someone I know? Of course it is, otherwise you would say—but someone who is not a gentleman?"

"Isabella, calm yourself," said Katarina as best she could. This had been a mistake; she never should have opened her mouth about the whole thing. "There *is* no man."

It took several minutes to convince her sister that there was no mysterious man who was about to whisk away her sister to an unequal marriage. Every minute of it, Katarina felt in some way that she was betraying Isaac and felt sick to her stomach.

Which was foolishness, she knew. What promises had he made her? None. What promises had she made him? None at all.

They had conversed for perhaps minutes. Katarina did not understand it, did not understand this desperate need to be close to him, to hear his voice. To be by his side. Could not comprehend where this certainty came from within her, that she needed to be with him.

That being with him was the only way that she could truly be happy.

"You really had me worried there for a moment," said Isabella, placing a hand on her chest and looking truly exhausted from the conversation, for which Katarina was sorry. "I thought you truly meant it!"

"Meant what?" asked Harmony.

Katarina shot a warning glance at her sister, but it arrived too late.

"Kitty here was teasing me about having met a man she was going to marry, even though he was not a gentleman!"

Roars of laughter and squeals echoed around the room as Katarina sighed and lowered her head. Perfect. That was precisely what she needed—her sister and cousins to spread such a rumor within the family. It would be believed, of course. It was just the sort of thing someone would expect her of doing.

The fact that she was, in actuality, far closer to falling in love with a man who their Papa would certainly not approve of...that was neither here nor there.

"Don't speak such nonsense, Isabella, I was merely asking what you thought Papa would do," Katarina managed to say. "Besides, wasn't it you who thought Olivia and Luke may have formed an attachment?"

"Olivia—Olivia and that friend of yours, Lord Kingsley?" asked Esther, eyes wide, and focus entirely distracted—just as Katarina had intended. "Goodness, do tell!"

"I am not sure of it," said Isabella awkwardly, shooting daggers at Katarina who chose to ignore them.

Well, what hypocrisy! After revealing their discussion about marrying an untitled gentleman without even a by-your-leave!

Katarina smiled with barely concealed relief as the conversation continued on about Olivia and Luke. It was a pack of nonsense, of course—she could not imagine anything less likely than Luke and Olivia wedding—but it removed her from their focus, which was precisely what she wanted.

After all, it was not as though Isaac and she had ever discussed matrimony. She already knew what he would say to such a thing—that she was a lady, and he, just a servant.

Katarina sighed. Just a servant. It was such a mediocre way of describing someone as handsome and as quick-witted as Isaac. There were not words to describe him.

And if she was not careful, she knew she would find herself very much in love.

CHAPTER FIVE

KATARINA HAD NEVER meant to get caught, of course.

Later that afternoon, just as she was tying up the laces of her winter boots by the back door, determined to go outside and find Isaac—or at the very least, speak to the dairymaids, who always had more interesting conversation than her sisters or cousins ever did—a voice echoed behind her that proved she had slipped up and made a mistake.

"Katarina Fitzroy, you cannot be thinking of going outside in this weather!"

Katarina looked up with a wry expression. "What, you mean the glorious wintery sunshine?"

Her father laughed dryly. "Well, it is cold out there, little one. I would hate for you to catch a head cold the day before the Christmas Eve ball. I know how much you enjoy dancing."

Katarina smiled as she straightened up by the back door, both her boots now fully laced. It was true, she did typically enjoy the chance to meet people who were not related to her by blood. It was what made Caroline so interesting; she was a step- or half-sister to their London Fitzroy cousins really, but to all intents and purposes, she was a Fitzroy.

The dancing was all very well. Katarina was neither a good dancer, like Olivia, nor a bad one, as Joy was. No rhythm in her at all.

It was the people, however, that endeared balls so to Katarina. But not today. Not this Christmas Eve ball. Not if Isaac could not be there.

"I will be quite well, Papa," Katarina said firmly, winding a scarf around her neck. Maria had embroidered little hearts and flowers along the edges, something she had not cared for, but she wore it all the same. "I am wrapped up, as you like to say, and I feel a little…a little hemmed in by all the people here."

Her father, William, leaned in conspiratorially. "Can you keep a secret?"

Katarina giggled, despite herself. No matter how much older she got, no matter how tall she had grown, her Papa was always her Papa. He always knew precisely how to make her smile.

"No," she said with a laugh. "Not if Isabella is determined to have it out of me!"

William laughed. "Well, I think the two of you can be trusted to keep it to yourselves. The truth is…I find myself a little hemmed in also."

Katarina stared. Her father—her Papa, the one who had invited all the family to visit for the festive Christmas season, had invited Luke Kingsley, and had announced a Christmas Eve …he of all people was starting to tire of the noise?

It did not make sense. William Fitzroy loved a gathering. He always had. It was one of her most abiding impressions of him—it was why Luke Kingsley and his parents had always visited so often.

Katarina blinked, attempting to take in this new information. It was times like these that she was reminded that her Papa was also quite another kind of man entirely. A husband. A friend. Someone who had his own thoughts, his own ideas, his own life before she had arrived.

Someone she still was getting to know on a somewhat equal footing.

"And that is why I say," her Papa continued with a twinkle in his eyes, "do not think I have not noticed you slipping away."

Heat seared Katarina's cheeks, and she swiftly dropped her gaze to look at the carpet and her boots.

Drat. Well, she had believed herself far cleverer than she actually was it appeared. At least, she had not thought anyone had noticed how often she had slipped away from family gatherings, the wreath making, the luncheons, the endless conversations about the same old topics…

She was not entirely sure how long everyone had been here, but it had been too long.

Or perhaps it was not long enough. Katarina clasped her hands before her and tried to stop her heart from beating frantically, but it was no use.

Because once the merriment was over, once Christmas was done with, Luke would leave. He would go home and take Isaac with him. Every moment the Fitzroys and Luke were here, their noise and busyness would mask—at least for most—the fact of her disappearance.

And the moment the entire party disbanded…

"I like a little fresh air," Katarina said aloud, conscious her father was waiting for a response, sure it was not the one he wanted. "I did not wish to disturb by announcing my departure. I am not Jemima."

Her father chuckled at that. "You know 'tis only Jemima's way. She must have the room always looking at her."

"And that is not my way," said Katarina eagerly. If only she could persuade him, make him see… "I wish only for some moments of quiet and calm, that is all, Papa. I will be at the ball, of course."

It was a small price to pay, she supposed, for the opportunity to disappear at will. To slip off to the barns, the cowsheds, the stables, in search of a man who made her heart flutter and her knees weak.

For the chance to be kissed by him again…

Her Papa was frowning. "There's something you are not telling me, isn't there, Kitty?"

Katarina swallowed. "I am doing nothing wrong, Papa."

Which was almost the truth. It was not a lie, at the very least, and so Katarina looked up into her father's eyes and tried to will him to understand.

William sighed. "And if I attempted to tell you off for constantly disappearing and avoiding your family, who have come so far to see you?"

"To see all of us," countered Katarina.

"You know what I mean, Katarina."

Kitty no more, it appeared. "If you order me to stay in the house, Papa, of course I will. But I would much rather go out when I wish, then be with the family when I wish. You would not like to force me, would you?"

Her father smiled with a slight frown. "You would not like me to have to, would you?"

That was the trouble with having such a clever man for a father, Katarina thought. He was rather too clever for his own good. Hers, too.

"We are going to be singing carols around the pianoforte," said her Papa with a knowing look. "Harmony has agreed to play for us."

"Well, that's a relief," Katarina said with a snort of laughter. "Poor old Isabella is not to be trusted."

"That is unkind and not the point," her father said gently. "Will you join us?"

Katarina hesitated. She turned away from her father and looked through the small window just to the right of the back door.

Carols with her family, half of them out of tune, and Harmony and Esther trying desperately to keep them all together…or a conversation with Isaac, a servant who would be gone in a matter of days, and who may just kiss her?

It was not really a choice.

"How lovely for you to enjoy Harmony's playing," Katarina said brightly. "You will have to tell me all about it later."

"Kitty—"

"Tell me about it at dinner, Papa!" Katarina shouted over her shoulder as she opened up the back door, stepped through it, and slammed it shut.

She started marching away before he could open it and call her back. He was right; she would not be able to resist a direct order, not from her Papa, but at the same time, she was desperate to see Isaac.

Isaac Emmett. There was a man who fascinated her. There was something about him, something she did not understand. Something she could not understand.

It did not take her long to find him. Katarina poked her nose into the cowshed for a moment but saw only the afternoon milking taking place.

"He's in the stables," said one of the maids a milking.

Katarina flushed. It was bad enough that her father had noticed her disappearances—now the maids knew she was looking for Isaac?

The maid giggled. "He was looking for you earlier, I figured he left a note at the house for you to look in on him. Or not. Whichever, he is in the stables."

The heat that tinged Katarina's cheeks increased, and she quickly removed her head from the door. Isaac had been looking for her? Why? What could he possibly have to say to her that would merit him asking after her to the milkmaids?

Swallowing down her questions and hoping she had not made too much of a fool of herself, Katarina skirted around the edge of the cowshed and reached her hand out to the door—but before she opened it, she hesitated.

What sort of nonsense was she getting herself tangled into? Was it possible that this was not only a poor idea, but one that she would regret?

These were not the actions, after all, of a well-bred lady. Katarina hardly knew what had got into her, but it was something quite different from anything she had ever experienced. But what was the alternative?

The idea of returning back to the house, of standing alongside her sisters and cousins singing dreary carol after dreary carol soared into her mind. Katarina took a deep breath. She would rather face the unknown consequences of what meeting with Isaac Emmett meant.

The stables were warm, far warmer than outside. Katarina could feel her shoulders relax as she stepped inside and closed the doors behind her. For some reason, she could not imagine anything bad happening inside stables. They just felt...warm. Safe.

"You just cannot stay away, can you?"

Katarina beamed at the man standing on the other end of the stables, pitchfork in one hand, smile on his face.

Isaac Emmett. The entirety of the day's struggles seemed to melt away as she looked at him. What was this sensation, when merely looking at a person removed such tension in one's neck?

She may not understand it, but that did not mean she did not want it. Very much.

"Neither can you," she said lightly, stepping forward.

Isaac raised an eyebrow. "Now what is that supposed to mean?"

Katarina's smile grew. "I heard from one of the maids a milking. You were looking for me earlier, weren't you?"

Was that a tinge of pink on his cheeks? Katarina could not tell; the moment she had spoken those words, Isaac turned away from her and returned to the chore he had evidently been hard at work at before she had entered.

Another hay bale was lifted up into the hayloft above the stalls where Hedge, Bramble, and the Chalcroft horses were gently nickering.

"I have no idea what you are talking about."

"Of course," Katarina said smoothly, belying the rapidly fluttering heart in her chest. This was foolish. He was just a man. They were just having a conversation. "You did not ask the milking maids where I was. You were not looking for me at all."

How was it possible that she could speak so smoothly when her whole being seemed on edge, ready to spring into action, though to do what, Katarina had no idea.

The last time she had seen Isaac, he had been kissing her rather passionately against a wall.

Katarina swallowed. No matter how much she wanted him to do that again, she would not ask for it. She was no common milkmaid!

"Well, so what if I was?" came the rather terse reply.

Katarina leaned against the wall, just a few feet from him. "Well, that would be nice."

Her words were soft, and perhaps it was the gentleness of her tone that made Isaac halt his efforts and turn to her.

She swallowed. Wearing naught but breeches and a shirt, a shirt moreover that was open at the top with no cravat and whose sleeves were rolled up…

It was a marvelously delightful picture. One she would not be able to forget in a hurry.

"You were with your family, I was told at the backdoor," Isaac said quietly, leaning. "Quite sternly, I might add. I saw no reason to disturb you from your family."

Katarina smiled shyly. "You should have done."

Why was it that she could not stop looking at him? If she looked away, she was certain, Isaac would disappear in a puff of smoke. He was too perfect. Too handsome to be allowed.

"Now why would a young lady such as yourself say a thing like that?" Isaac said with a raised eyebrow. "There's many a person in this world who would be grateful for such a family as yours."

"How do you know?" asked Katarina curiously. "What has Luke said about us?"

"Oh, Luke says nothing much," Isaac said with a wave of his hand.

Katarina looked at him. Luke. That was strange. A mere

carriage driver was not usually on first name speaking terms with their master, were they?

"Besides," he added, turning to put another hay bale up in the hayloft. "One does not need to know much about your family to know they are good people."

"You speak as though you know much of the opposite." Katarina was not entirely sure what made her say those words, but it was clear in every inch of him that he did.

Isaac was on edge. There was a tension in him, a tautness that appeared whenever he spoke of her family. What had happened with his own family, Katarina wondered. Was he estranged from them, perhaps?

He sighed heavily, stuck the pitchfork in the straw, and turned to her. "You're not going to leave me alone, are you?"

"Do you want me to?" Katarina had not intended to be a flirt, but she saw with surprise and more than a little pleasure that her words had quite an effect on the coachman.

Isaac's neck pinked slightly. "No. Damnit, woman, you know I like your company."

Pleasure rushed through Katarina's heart. Did he know, could he possibly know how much joy his words had just given her? Was this all in her mind, a fancy that her sister Olivia would certainly call "passing"—or was this something else? Something deeper?

And how on earth would she tell the difference?

"Tell me about them," Katarina said quietly. "Your family."

A nerve twitched in Isaac's jaw. "Not much to tell, I suppose. I argued with my father years ago, an argument that was partly my fault, but in my opinion, mostly his own, and from that moment he wished to have nothing to do with me. And we have not."

Katarina could not help but be amazed at the terseness of his tone. There was true pain there. He had been hurt, cast off by his father, and by no more than a mere argument.

She shivered. If her father were like that, so easy to break with his child…why, the Fitzroy sisters had more than enough debates between themselves, let alone with their parents. But perhaps it was different with sons.

"You have not seen him in all that time?" she asked quietly.

"Six years," said Isaac, a shadow passing across his face. "And so, I entered the world with little credit to my name save my honesty and my desire to work hard."

Katarina swallowed and tried not to look at the greatest evidence of that hard work that she was presented with in that moment, the sweat on his brow, the strength of his arms. Arms that had held her against a wall as she had threatened to fall from the overwhelming pressure of his ardor.

"I...I am impressed."

Isaac snorted. "I did not say it to impress you."

"I know. That is why I am impressed." Katarina laughed as she saw his expression. "No, truly. If you had attempted to impress me, you would have told me the topic of your argument, tried to convince me that you were the one in the right. But you did not."

There was a rather astounded look on Isaac's face. "You are rather a clever woman, you know that?"

"I do indeed," said Katarina with a laugh. "Although...although I am not sure I am clever when I am with you."

Isaac took a step forward. "Is that right?"

Katarina shook her head. This was foolishness, she knew. Not merely foolishness but recklessness. This was the sort of harlot behavior that she would expect of a woman with no good name and no prospects, not of a Fitzroy of Chalcroft.

Yet reason was fast disappearing as Isaac approached her. There was something about him. She trusted him, she wanted him, she knew him and yet wanted to know him.

There was such complexity in his eyes, such interest in his mind. Katarina wanted to spend all day with him here in the safety and warmth of the stables, just...talking to him. Learning about him. Hearing his opinion on the world and sharing her own.

And kissing. Katarina shivered.

"I know precisely what you are thinking," said Isaac in a low voice as he stopped right before her.

Katarina longed to close the gap between them but knew it was certainly not her place to do such a thing. She was a young lady, though she was losing all sense of respectability each moment that Isaac stood before her, all man, heat, and desire.

"You do?"

Isaac nodded. "You want to kiss me, don't you?"

Katarina wet her lips, and he groaned. "And you want to kiss me, don't you?"

"More than anything," said Isaac in a low voice. "But Kat—this is a mistake."

Kat. Katarina shivered. No one had ever called her that before. She rather liked it. She liked the way he just created a name for her without asking, without inquiring. Just a name between the two of them.

"A mistake?" she repeated, looking deep into his eyes and wondering what it would be like to be held in those arms without the support of a wall.

Isaac sighed. "You are a lady, I am...a servant. There is more that divides us than unites us. I...I cannot offer you anything, even if I wanted to. I belong here in the stables, and you belong up there in that big fancy ball you have tomorrow evening."

Katarina hesitated. He was right. There was not a single word he said that she could refute. This was foolish. It could very easily be a mistake.

And yet she knew deep within herself that not taking this chance of happiness, of pleasure, no matter how long it lasted, would be the true mistake. One she would regret for the rest of her life.

"I just want to talk," she said breathlessly, a complete lie. "Just talk, Isaac."

"Just talk?" Isaac closed the gap, pulling her with a gasp into his arms before inhaling just below her ear and placing a delicate kiss on her neck, his hands slowly lowering to her buttocks. "And is that all you want?"

Katarina could barely think, let alone speak. So many heady sensations she had never experienced before were clouding her judgement. Because it would always be yes. Always be him.

"Talk to me," she managed.

Isaac kissed her again on the neck, then released her.

The separation was so unexpected, Katarina almost fell. Strong arms reached out to steady her.

"I do not think you are ready for just talk, if just talk leads to just kissing, and just kissing leads to…dear God, woman, don't look at me like that," said Isaac with a knowing smile that made Katarina blush. "So how about you and I sit here a while and discuss things."

Katarina raised an eyebrow. "Discuss things?"

"*Actually* discuss things," Isaac said with a laugh. "Three feet apart at all times. And no funny business, Miss Kat, I know all the stories of ladies from big houses seducing poor young men such as myself."

Katarina laughed as she half sat, half fell onto a hay bale. She could not think of anything less likely. It was Isaac who had all the power in this scenario, Isaac who could do anything to her as long as he kissed her—Isaac, she knew, who was the one who could tell her to leave him or…to leave with him.

She swallowed. That was madness. A man she met only a few days ago, and she was already considering elopement?

But it did happen every day, she thought as Isaac effortlessly picked up a bale of hay and placed it before hers—at least three feet apart. At least, people met at balls or card parties or the like, and the decision was made that they liked each other, and that was that. They wed.

Was this really so different?

"Now," Isaac said impressively, pulling out a golden pocket watch which appeared far too impressive for a mere coachman. "You have two…maybe just over two hours of my time. How would you like to spend it? What would you like to discuss?"

He looked up and smiled, and Katarina absolutely melted. "Everything."

CHAPTER SIX

"I THEREFORE CONSIDER this Christmas Eve ball—open!"

Cheers rang out in the great hall as William Fitzroy opened the front doors to allow the waiting guests entrance.

Katarina looked around. There were flushed, excited faces on Isabella and Lucy's faces, while Esther was patting down her skirts, trying to make sure that her gown was hanging properly. Jemima was hurriedly speaking with Harmony about something that surely could not be that interesting, while Olivia simply watched, a thoughtful look on her face that usually meant trouble.

Katarina sighed. Such a palaver, and for what? A few neighbors to turn up and dance a few merry jigs. The entire Fitzroy cousins would be expected to open the dancing, which was as it should be, but beyond that...

As the guests poured into Chalcroft, her father beamed at the many new faces. "Come on through, come on through. We have music and dancing in the ballroom, food put out in the dining room—yes, of course there is roast lamb..."

It was strange. Now that Katarina knew her father sometimes put a smile on for appearances, it was rather odd to watch him welcome their guests. Was he actually happy to see them? Or was he merely playing the perfect role as the host?

Perhaps the whole world was like that. Perhaps almost all of them were going around pretending, and not telling anyone what they really thought.

It was a heady idea. It almost meant Katarina missed part of an argument going on behind her.

"You should have plenty of partners for the dancing," Olivia said with a smile to their cousin Joy.

But Joy did not appear pleased by the pronouncement. On the contrary, her cheeks flushed scarlet, and when she spoke, it was in a hurried, anguished whisper. "I did not ask—I am not desperate for partners, Olivia, and I hope you will not say that I am so! I merely remarked on the number of gentlemen!"

She stormed away in the direction of the dining room, leaving Olivia, as far as Katarina could see, utterly at a loss.

Well, that was the trouble with Fitzroys in a large group, Katarina thought wryly. There was always so much going on, so much emotion. It was easy, sometimes, to offend—even without meaning to.

"Please, come on into the ballroom," Olivia said loudly to the chattering crowd as though the offense against Joy had never happened.

Katarina scowled. She was always acting like their mother. Perhaps it was part of being the eldest, but she wasn't sure about that. Olivia enjoyed it. There was no other reason for her to be so...so forceful.

So lost in her thoughts, Katarina had not noticed her eldest sister walking toward her—and by the time she did notice, it was too late.

"You know, I do not think I have seen you these last three days together," Olivia said as she reached Katarina, leaning against the wall by the door to the ballroom. "Where on earth have you been, Kitty?"

Katarina glared. "Mind your own business."

She probably should not have been so direct, but she couldn't help it. There had been enough demands that Katarina stay in the house, entertaining her cousins, and she was tired of it. What did it matter to everyone else where she went? She was not hurting anyone, was she?

And her conversations with Isaac…they were magical. Katarina had never known someone with such emotions, such wit—such intelligence. Isaac must not spend that much time working as a coachman for Luke; he must read a great deal. His mind was more alive to the possibilities of the world than anyone else she had ever met.

Unfortunately, her rudeness made Olivia halt in her tracks and stare at her sister most wondrously. "I beg your pardon?"

Katarina knew she should not give into the temptation to be rude again—it was quite unnecessary, and Olivia did not deserve to be shouted at merely because Isaac had not been invited to the Christmas Eve ball.

Not for her lack of trying, however.

"I really think you should invite the servants," she had said to their father just a few hours ago.

William had snorted. "The servants?"

"Yes!" Katarina said earnestly as her Papa ordered the final decorations of the ballroom under her mother's watchful eye. "It is their Christmas, too, I do not see why they cannot join the celebrations."

Her heart had pattered most uncomfortably at that. The idea of Isaac joining them, of being able to see him in a formal jacket and breeches, and being held in his arms as they danced down the line…

"Absolutely not," her Papa said firmly.

Katarina had frowned. "Why on earth not?"

"The servants have Boxing Day all to themselves, and that is far more than many get," said her Papa. "Besides, do you not think that we will need servants to be working to host the ball? Who do you think will be serving punch, welcoming guests, organizing the food?"

Katarina had bit her lip. She had not considered such things. "What about the gardeners then—or the stable hands or the milkmaids—"

"Milkmaids?" William halted at that point to stare at his daughter. "Katarina, what has got into you? Are you feeling quite well?"

And Katarina had sighed and given it up. She could not force her father to accept Isaac to the ball, and that did not bode well for her future hopes. If William Fitzroy did not want a coachman or a milkmaid dancing at his Christmas Eve ball, what would he think of the idea of having one as a son-in-law?

Katarina swallowed. Olivia was still staring at her as guests poured into the ballroom. "I said mind your own business, and leave your nose out of mine."

It was still not enough to force her sister to leave her alone. In fact, Olivia's eyes narrowed, and she took a step toward her and spoke low, to prevent others from hearing their conversation.

"Kitty," said Olivia so quietly that Katarina had to step forward to hear her. "You…you do know that you can come to me with anything, you know that?"

Katarina tried to keep herself calm, but it was no use. Heat flushed her cheeks, and she looked down to avoid her sister's gaze. Olivia was the last person she wished to speak to about Isaac. She wouldn't understand. All she thought about was rank and prestige, all that nonsense. She probably wouldn't even give Isaac a polite smile.

"This is…this isn't…'tis nothing to do with you."

If only she could find the words to convince her sister, but Katarina could see, even in her own embarrassment, that Olivia was not convinced.

She should never have even come to the ball. Katarina should have pled a headache, stayed upstairs—or even crept out of the house and spent the evening talking to Isaac. That would have been an evening far better spent. Kissing Isaac…

"Katarina Fitzroy," Olivia said in almost a whisper. "You haven't…you would not…there have been no interactions with a g-gentleman that you want to tell me about, are there?"

All Katarina's warmth drained from her—it was her very worst nightmare. She had never considered that anyone in her family would have guessed her affection for Isaac, even after her rather awkward conversation with Isabella. Though still attempting to untangle in her own mind how she felt about him, Katarina knew it was an emotion deeper than anything she felt for any other.

And Olivia...Olivia had found out!

Katarina swallowed, trying to stay calm, but her stomach swooped most painfully. "Who—who told you?"

"What are you two doing here, standing at the sidelines?" Their cousin Lucy had appeared out of nowhere, a huge smile on her face, and seemingly unable to notice the tension between the two sisters, placed her hands on Olivia and Katarina's shoulders. "This is your house, your Christmas Eve ball! The dancing is about to begin! Come on!"

Katarina had no choice but to enter the ballroom with Olivia and Lucy, though both drifted away almost immediately to talk to others, leaving her alone.

Which was what she needed. Her mind was racing so fast that Katarina could barely take in what was going on around her. The ballroom was becoming more and more packed—it would soon become a crush if they were not careful. How like her Papa to invite far too many people; not that it sounded like people were disappointed to receive an invitation...

"A short journey really, and one has an invitation from William Fitzroy—"

"—just as I had always thought it would look, and, of course, receiving an invitation to Chalcroft is such an honor..."

Katarina smiled weakly at those speaking as she rushed past them. She had to sit down—but almost every seat at the sides were already taken.

She was warm—too warm. Her gown was not particularly thick, a light silk, but after her conversation with Olivia, Katarina felt far too hot. Her stays pinched at her sides.

"Katarina Fitzroy. You haven't...you would not...there have been no interactions with a g-gentleman that you want to tell me about, are there?"

Katarina swallowed, putting a hand to her chest to feel the awkward pattering of her heart. Well, she should probably take some solace that her sister considered Isaac a gentleman, even if her father would consider him a mere servant.

What was it that Isabella said?

"Truly, you have met someone with whom you have fallen in love? You have decided on him, that he will make you happy, even if he breaks our father's heart?"

Head spinning, not knowing whether to run upstairs and hide herself away, or creep out of the house and find Isaac, tell him what he was starting to mean to her, Katarina found herself by the punch table.

"You look quite done in," said a cheerful voice.

Katarina blinked. Luke Kingsley was standing there in a rather extravagant cravat and a smile, a smile that disappeared the longer he looked at her.

"Kitty," he said quietly, taking a step toward her and speaking low. "Are you feeling well?"

Katarina tried to consider how she could explain the whole thing without giving away any details which were important, but for some reason, she gave up almost immediately.

She could trust Luke, couldn't she? He was a gentleman, a man of the world. He had surely seen unequal marriages, heard of scandals like this, and would be a little more worldly than her irritating sister, Olivia.

He would not betray her—and he knew Isaac, would know if he had ever...well. Katarina did not even like to consider it, but still, she had to face it. Was this something that Isaac had done before with other ladies when Luke had visited other people? Was she, in fact, just one in a long line?

"It's Isaac," she breathed.

Luke took her hand in his. "Breathe, Kitty, you look pale as anything. Say that again—did you say Isaac?"

Katarina nodded miserably. How could she explain? It was all so ridiculous—she had managed to allow herself to fall in love with a man who was so far removed from her...what was the likelihood of it ever working? She could not imagine a world in which they could be happy together.

But she wanted to be. She wanted to be with Isaac.

"Isaac Emmett," she said in a low voice, hardly able to look Luke in the eyes. His hand was comforting around hers, steadying her as the room spun. "Your coachman."

"My—*that* Isaac?" Luke said in a slightly wondrous voice. "Oh. Ah."

Katarina nodded helplessly. "And it is all so complicated, and I do not even know if he wishes to—and my father would never—"

"Miss Fitzroy."

Katarina and Luke looked up. They had been so absorbed in their conversation that it appeared neither of them had noticed the gentleman in a rather splendid crimson jacket and waistcoat approach them. He was smiling broadly.

"Miss Fitzroy, may I have this first dance?"

Katarina blinked at him. Dance? She had not even considered dancing, not if Isaac could not be here. What would be the point?

Instinctively, she looked up at Luke as she would a brother.

"I am so terribly sorry, old thing, but Miss Katarina has already agreed to dance the first with me," said Luke smoothly.

The gentleman looked disappointed but bowed his head and departed.

"Thank you," breathed Katarina.

Luke sighed heavily and shook his head with a rueful smile. "The dash of it all is that I had wanted to dance with...but no matter. We will have to do it now, and you can tell me—"

"Let the dancing, begin!"

Katarina glanced at her father, who had made the pronouncement as the musicians struck up their notes. Lucy was once again full of excitement; Katarina could see her pulling

Isabella to the center of the room with one hand, and a rather reticent looking Maria with the other.

"Shall we?"

Katarina looked back at Luke, who was smiling and offering his arm. He had wanted to dance with someone else, she thought, his words catching up with her. Who? Which young lady had he asked her father to invite so that he could dance with her?

Still, it made no difference now. She tried to plaster a smile on her face. "We shall."

Katarina could not think of anything she wanted to do less than join her sisters and cousins in the center of the ballroom with their partners, standing in a long line ready for the musicians to begin the dance.

It was only when the music began and Luke stepped toward her to bow, along with the other gentlemen in the set, that Katarina noticed that with two of her sisters, all her cousins, and a lady she did not recognize, there were nine ladies dancing.

But none of them were Olivia. She was standing at the side, glaring most strangely at Katarina.

Katarina blinked. Surely it was a trick of the light, a strange coincidence based on the way she was standing.

But no. As she and Luke moved down the set, Olivia's angry gaze followed them. What on earth did it mean?

"So," said Luke quietly as they came together in the dance. "Isaac."

Katarina flushed. "You do not think ill of me?"

"I would have done if I thought ill of him," countered Luke with a wry smile. "I do not pretend your path will be easy. Has Isaac spoke of...of the future?"

Katarina shook her head. "No, I...I haven't been brave enough to do that yet. I mean, a servant! Papa would never countenance such a thing."

Was that a knowing smile on Luke's face? "Well, I think there are probably a few things that he needs to talk to you about before conversation of the future can begin. If you do not mind me being so bold, Kitty."

Katarina stared. What did he know about Isaac that she did not? There was evidently something, for there was such a strange look on Luke's face that did not make sense. Was there a great secret about his coachman that she should know?

"Luke," she began in a low voice, "tell me—"

"Olivia!" Luke said as the dance halted for them for a moment. "You are not dancing."

"No, it appears not," Olivia said in a sharp voice.

Katarina could not understand it. There was no reason for her sister not to dance; there was plenty of room, and nine couples was a rather awkward number.

It appeared Luke was very much of her own mind. "Well, why on earth not?" he asked with a grin. "It's marvelous fun!"

"How—how dare you speak to me like that after what you have said and done," Olivia hissed, loudly enough for Katarina to hear, who stared at her sister. Olivia appeared genuinely upset, though she could not see what Luke could have done, of all people. "How dare you accept my attentions, tease me, tempt me along a path that I—and you were interested in Kitty all along!"

Katarina almost laughed aloud. So, was that what Olivia had got herself all worked up about? She thought Luke—*Luke*—was interested in her?

"Kitty—Katarina, you mean?" Luke said, equally as astonished. "Olivia, you do not understand—"

The conversation continued, hissed between them under the music, but Katarina was no longer listening. She could not. She had been utterly distracted by a face at the window.

Isaac's face. He was staring in at the spectacle of the ball, and in that moment his gaze met hers. Something shot through them, something powerful, like lightning, but far more warming.

Katarina stepped away from the dance instinctively, without a second thought. What care she for a silly old dance when Isaac was just there?

His eyes widened, and he disappeared at once from the window. It did not matter. Katarina knew precisely where he had gone, and it did not take her long to push past the crowds who were now applauding the musicians, out into the great hall, which was still crowded with people, and out of the front door.

Cries called after her.

"Miss Fitzroy, where are you—"

"Wasn't that one of the Fitzroy ladies?"

"I can barely tell them apart you know, there are so many..."

Katarina ignored them all. Despite the icy wind, she strode purposefully toward the stables, throwing open the door.

He was not there.

Breathing heavily, determined to find him, knowing she had to speak with him and understand him, Katarina thought quickly. Where else could Isaac be?

The cowshed was just as warm as the stables, with the eight milkmaids gathered at one end, conversing and laughing—but Katarina was not interested in them. Her gaze moved until she finally saw what she was looking for.

Isaac Emmett. In a towering temper, by the look of him, seated at the other end of the cowshed to the milkmaids.

"Isaac," Katarina breathed, almost running toward him. She did not care if the milk-maids were watching her; the whole world could watch her, for all she cared. Her affection for Isaac was not something to be hidden, but to be celebrated.

"Isaac," she repeated as she reached him.

"Miss Fitzroy," Isaac said stiffly, inclining his head.

It was such a frosty reception that at first, Katarina hesitated, wondering whether she should take a step back, leave him in peace—but the desire that welled up as she looked at him forced her forward. She would speak with him; she would know.

"I-I saw you looking in at the window," she said as the laughter of the milkmaids echoed around the cowshed. "Why did you not come in?"

"Come in?" Isaac laughed dryly as he looked up at her, fierceness in his gaze. "Katarina Fitzroy, you simply do not understand—we are so different, you and I! Different worlds, worlds that should never have…"

His voice trailed away, and Katarina's stomach twisted painfully. Should never have come together. That was what he was going to say, she knew it.

"I do not believe that," she said quietly. "I feel as though my world only makes sense when I am near you."

Isaac swallowed but did not look away from her. Katarina smiled hesitantly, hoping he could see in her the love she was starting to feel for him. Could he not see it? Sometimes she felt it was so obvious it would burst from her.

"You do not understand," he said finally. "And you never could. You do not have the bravery to step outside your world, Katarina, and into mine. Not truly."

Katarina's mouth fell open. He could say that to her—to her face? It was intolerable. Though fear was certainly pattering through her heart, it was easily overwhelmed by passion, and desire—and a decision she was about to make that would change her life forever.

"Out," she said quietly.

Isaac raised an eyebrow. "I beg your pardon?"

"Out," Katarina said loudly, but this time she turned away from him and looked at the milkmaids. "All of you, out!"

CHAPTER SEVEN

KATARINA WAS SHAKING, and she did not know why.

The very first moment she had seen Isaac Emmett she had known he would be a special part of her life. Knew she needed him, needed him in a way that was entirely new.

Katarina did not take her eyes from Isaac as the last milkmaid left the cowshed, and he did not look away from her.

What was it in his eyes? She could barely tell. Part fury, though she knew not why; part desire, which she hoped was not her imagination; part confusion as to why she had ordered away the milkmaids.

Katarina barely knew herself. Except that she had to be alone with him. She had to speak to him openly in the way they had the other day. When she had barely been able to hear her own words over the frantic beating of her heart.

The door closed heavily behind her.

"Well," said Isaac expressively, widening his arms. "Now we are alone—is that what you wanted?"

"Yes," Katarina said simply.

The man sighed heavily. "May I speak plainly, Miss Katarina?"

"Only if you call me Kat again."

A wry smile crept across Isaac's face. "My dear, if I could call you all the things I wanted…"

His voice trailed away, but there was no fury within it now.

Katarina moved toward him and was heartened that he did not pull away.

Seating herself beside him, highly conscious of the heat she could feel in his arms as hers brushed up against his own, Katarina tried to slow her breathing.

She was just having a conversation. That was all. The family, all of them, were occupied with the ball and would not be looking for her for many hours. They would assume, wouldn't they, that she was dancing elsewhere, or eating from the buffet in the dining room, or adjusting her gown.

She had all night. All night with Isaac.

A shiver rushed through her before Katarina could stop it.

"What's on that mind of yours?"

Katarina smiled ruefully. "I am not sure I should tell you."

Isaac chuckled at her words. "And even worse, I did not call you Kat. You will have to ignore my request altogether."

She laughed, feeling the joy in him as he moved closer to her. Katarina could not remember ever sitting this close to a gentleman she was not related to. Luke did not count.

"Even if you do not think you should share them, Kat," came Isaac's soft words, "What are you thinking?"

Katarina sighed. It would be so easy to lie; if anyone else had asked, she probably would have done. But lying to Isaac felt wrong in a way that nothing else did.

"Thinking of you," she said, a little wistfully. "At least— thinking about you and Luke."

Isaac shook his head. "Two very different men."

"That's just it," said Katarina quietly. "Yes, you are different I suppose, in some ways. Luke has a title, wealth, all that non-sense—but I feel equally as comfortable in each of your presences. And he doesn't make me feel...feel warm."

Her cheeks flushed slightly as she spoke, but she told herself that was natural. She had never spoken of these feelings before, to anyone—had never had these feelings before.

All of this was so new, and she was glad to be sharing it with him.

"You see similarities, but I see only differences," said Isaac with a heavy sigh. "Luke is a nobleman, really. Beyond my position, beyond gentry. When he marries, it will be for wealth or prestige or love. He has that choice. A choice many of us do not have."

Katarina's breath caught in her throat. Was Isaac trying to tell her—was he attempting to say that he wished he was free, free to make such a free choice…but was not?

She swallowed. "We are the same in that regard, then."

Isaac snorted. "Oh, come, Kat, do not treat me like a child."

"I am not!" protested Katarina, her eyes wide. How could he not see it—it was so obvious to her.

"You truly think we are that alike?" asked Isaac quietly. "You are a lady, well-born, gentry born. You live in a manor! Your biggest concerns are whether you will enjoy the music at a concert you go to in Bath, or, or if a gown style comes in your favorite silk!"

"You do not know me at all if you think me that frivolous and empty-headed!" Katarina said with a laugh, though a prickle of discomfort seared through her heart. Well, he was not entirely wrong. Not for all the Fitzroy sisters. Olivia, for example… "But yes, I see similarities. You say you do not have choice in your marriage—well, neither do I."

Even seated beside him, Katarina could see Isaac raise an unimpressed eyebrow.

"I mean it!" she said hotly. "I am a lady, yes, but that gives me less power of choice over the man I marry than—than Molly the milkmaid! She may marry for love, whereas I must make alliances if I am to please my father. You and I, even if we…we met someone we cared for…it would be difficult."

Katarina's words ended lamely, and she dropped her gaze to her hands in her lap.

Why was it so difficult to express herself? So many thoughts and emotions were whirling around her mind, it was quite a job to catch a single one.

And this was Isaac, a man who made her heart spin and her body ache for his touch. A man who kissed her so passionately, she was surprised he had held back from there.

If only he had not…

Katarina flushed. It was not seemly for a lady to desire such things, she knew; but she was not made of ice, but fire. She wanted to burn with the passion between them, to fulfill this aching need within her that grew each moment she was with him.

"Perhaps you are right," came Isaac's quiet voice. "But Kat, you and I live in separate worlds. Do you not think that a part of you is only interested in me because of that? I mean, that you wish to rebel against your father as much as you wish to kiss me?"

Katarina twisted to look directly at Isaac. It was not something she had considered before, and now he had said it so solemnly, she wanted to consider it carefully.

She looked at him. Dark, serious eyes; a mouth that begged to be kissed, that seemed to be calling out to her; a heart that was generous, interesting, warm.

And she knew in that moment. Whether or not her father approved of Isaac, he was the man she wanted to be with. There was nothing she wanted more than to be with him, to be his. Wife, mistress, lover…Katarina was not even sure whether that mattered any more.

"I want you," she said softly, gazing straight into his eyes. "I…I cannot pretend it is not exciting to think that we come from such different worlds, but that is not why…you do something to me, Isaac, something I do not understand. Something I cannot explain. Something that makes me want to throw all caution to the wind and do whatever I want, regardless of society."

Isaac smiled, his gaze darting down to her mouth. "Is that so?"

His hands moved to hers, clasping them in her lap, and Katarina shivered with the intensity of such a small gesture.

When one was rarely touched by another, when even taking someone's hand in a dance was heightened with danger and intrigue, sitting here with Isaac alone, hand in hand, was intoxicating. Katarina could feel the desire rushing through her veins, pouring into her, growing with each passing moment.

"Kiss me," she whispered.

It appeared Isaac was waiting only for her invitation. Leaning forward, Isaac crushed his lips onto hers, giving Katarina the sweet relief she was crying out for, releasing the tension within her.

His lips were warm, his kiss tender, but it deepened as Katarina broke free of his hands and placed her own around his neck. She wanted to be as close to him as possible, to feel him in a way she never had done before.

There was something heady about simply sitting beside him and kissing Isaac. Katarina lost herself in the kiss, her senses falling away from the cowshed, the warm musty smell of it, to focus entirely on Isaac.

His taste, his power as his tongue teased her own, the way his hands had moved to her shoulders to bring her closer.

And she wanted more. Katarina had never known desire like this, passion like this. Every inch of her body tingled, desperate for his touch—desperate for everything he could give her.

The question was, was she brave enough to give it to him? Would she cast aside her concerns, and give herself to Isaac Emmett?

"Kat," Isaac groaned, pulling away from her but leaving his hands on her shoulders, almost possessively. "We should not be doing this."

"I quite agree," breathed Katarina as she leaned forward to kiss him again.

Isaac chuckled as the kiss began, but his ardor seemed to overwhelm him as the kiss continued.

It was only when his fumbling fingers started trying to pull down her gown over her shoulders that Katarina broke the kiss and looked, startled, into Isaac's eyes.

"I am sorry, I should not…" Isaac took a deep, shuddering breath. "I am finding it hard to keep my hands off you, Kat, and I should—it's important to me that you can trust me."

Katarina knew what he needed to hear, though she said it through a haze of lust. "I do trust you."

Isaac looked at her with a wry smile. "You do, do you?"

She nodded. There was no one else in the world that she trusted so much as the man sitting before her in this moment. Isaac Emmett was a man to trust, whether he was a gentleman or not.

"How much?"

Katarina swallowed. Here she was, right on the edge of a precipice. Unsure exactly how she knew it, Katarina was quite certain that this was the moment that she could either choose to jump off the cliff into Isaac's waiting arms, or instead, retreat back to safety, toward the morals of society, back to what was expected of her.

Back to the house. Back to her old life. Back to Chalcroft and the Christmas Eve ball.

But she would always wonder, wouldn't she? Katarina felt the excitement grow in her stomach, then below her stomach, as the thought of what Isaac could mean grew in her heart.

She wanted him. She wanted him to kiss her, to kiss her all over.

"Completely," she breathed. "I trust you, Isaac, completely. Have your way with me."

Isaac's look of dark desire overshadowed his face for a moment, and then it was gone—and just reverence remained.

"You are so beautiful, Kat," he murmured, "inside and out. I want to show you just how beautiful."

And then he was kissing her, kissing her as he had done when he had pressed her up against the stable door—but it was different, somehow.

When Isaac had first kissed her, Katarina had known, somehow, that he would take things no further. That though he enjoyed kissing her, and she certainly squirmed with pleasure under his kisses, there was no more to be offered that day.

This was different. Isaac's kisses were no longer the destination, but a stepping stone toward something more glorious, more brilliant.

More intense than anything Katarina had ever known.

"Oh, Isaac," she breathed as his kisses started to trail down her neck, her head tilting back.

All she could do was accept the kisses, the pleasure he was giving her, her hands entangled in his hair, pulling him closer. She did not ever want to be apart from him. The idea of not sharing these kisses with him, these moments with him...it would be awful.

"Kat," Isaac groaned. "Come here."

She moved into his arms willingly, but she did not expect to be lifted bodily up from the hay bale. Laughing at the sudden movement, Katarina's lips were stopped with a kiss so deep and passionate, it spread tingles of pleasure throughout her body.

And then she was being laid carefully down onto the hay. Katarina looked up at Isaac with lust in her eyes, no longer caring whether he saw it or not. He had the right to know; Isaac deserved to know how much she wanted him.

"Come here," she said, lifting a hand to him.

Isaac had joined her in the hay before Katarina was able to say another word. She welcomed him into her arms, felt the weight of him, exalted in the connection they shared.

"Katarina," he murmured. "You are so beautiful."

She heard the words, but more importantly, she felt the truth of them in the way he touched her body. His fingers moved to her breasts, tenderly caressing them in a way that made Katarina shiver, arching her back into his touch, while his lips delicately brushed across her décolletage.

Katarina was unsure what she was supposed to be doing, but that did not matter. Her instincts took over.

"Love me," said Katarina desperately, hardly knowing what she was asking but knowing it was all she wanted.

Isaac halted. Looking down at her with wide yet loving eyes, he examined her closely for a few heart-stopping moments.

Katarina swallowed, wetting her lips. She could not take back the request, not now—and besides, she did not want to. She wanted him. She wanted to give herself to him, give herself in a way that was irrevocable.

No other man would ever be like this for her, and Katarina wanted to show him that; show him that he was like no other.

"Isaac, I know I ask for much," she said breathlessly, looking up into his handsome face, her palms against his shirt. "But I...I mean it. I want you, want this, want everything you can give me."

Isaac groaned as he lowered his head to kiss her. "You don't know what you are asking for, Kat."

Perhaps she did not, not entirely—but Katarina was determined to prove to him that she was willing to learn. Hardly aware of her own daring, acting instinctively rather than thinking through the consequences of her actions, Katarina allowed one of her hands to meander down his chest—to the hardness that was struggling to break free of his breeches.

The effect was instantaneous. Drawing in breath rapidly and breaking off the kiss, Isaac looked at her with startled eyes.

"Kat—"

"Love me," she urged him, her fingers gently stroking his manhood through the material, adoring the effect it had on him. "Love me, Isaac, like—like I love you."

The words had slipped out before she could halt them, but Katarina realized the moment they were spoken that she did not want to.

She loved him. Love at first sight, true love, lust, desire...it was all a medley together. It was all true. She had never known a truth like it.

"Damn, Kat, you are tempting me too hard," Isaac said, resting himself above her on an elbow.

"Then don't resist," Katarina said, lifting up her face to be kissed. "Don't resist me, Isaac…please, give me what I want. Love me. P-Pleasure me."

That was perhaps the word that tipped him over the edge, as far as Katarina could see: pleasure.

With a groan, Isaac crushed his lips on hers, giving himself to her in a way he had not yet done. His hand moved to where hers was teasing him, but not to remove it, but to press her fingers tighter against his manhood, and Katarina obeyed the unspoken desire, her movements becoming stronger, more rhythmical.

And then her fingers were pushed away.

Katarina broke the kiss, trying to look into Isaac's face. "I-I have displeased you?"

"Quite the opposite," Isaac said with a wry smile, his breath jagged. "But now it's my turn to take control, Kat. Do you still trust me?"

Katarina nodded, the sensation of the hay below and around her sparking across her skin, which seemed to be heightened to all touches.

It took Isaac but a moment to unbutton his breeches. Katarina only had a moment to stare at his manhood, amazed that something she had only seen on Greek and Roman statues was right there, before Isaac was gently pushing up her skirts.

But Katarina did not want gentle or slow—not now. Every part of her was crying out for him, for the completion of whatever came next, and Katarina's fingers scrabbled to join his, pulling her skirts above her knees, above her hips, revealing all of herself.

Isaac groaned. "Christ alive, Kat, you are not wearing any undershifts!"

Katarina grinned up at him, feeling mischievous and vixen-like. "I know."

"But how did you—"

"I just knew," she told him, pulling him back into his arms

and feeling the press of his manhood against her thigh, shivering at the anticipation of it all. "I just—Isaac!"

He had taken the moment while she was not entirely concentrating to enter her—and Katarina in that moment knew she would never give herself to another man, not ever.

After such a connection, such intimacy—she felt him move within her, felt the weight of him, the pressure of him, felt him filling her more and more, more than she could have imagined possible—and already the tendrils of pleasure were flickering throughout her body.

"Isaac," she said in wonder.

Isaac kissed her lightly on the lips. "Ready?"

Katarina stared up at him. "There—there's more?"

He chucked as he nuzzled her, one hand propping him up, one hand starting to tease her breast. "So, so much more."

It happened all at once and altogether, and Katarina arched her back with the unendurable pleasure of it all. Isaac had almost removed his manhood from her and then thrust back into her in a sweeping motion—just as his fingers had tightened around her breast, his thumb grazing her nipple through the thin silken fabric.

"Isaac!"

"I know," Isaac said in a low voice, kissing her neck, making Katarina almost giddy with pleasure as it rushed through her body. "Tell me if you want more."

"More?" Katarina gasped, and then cried out as he thrust into her again. "More, more, more!"

All thoughts as to whether someone may hear them disappeared as Katarina succumbed to the intensity of the ecstasy that was building inside her, every inch of her body wanting more.

Her legs twitched, her whole body squirmed as Isaac thrust into her with increasing pace, and suddenly Katarina could feel where they were going, and cried out the only thing she could think of.

"Isaac!"

He looked into her eyes and whispered, "More?"

"More!"

And Katarina exploded, as more pleasure than she could possibly have imagined rocked through her body. Her limbs shook, and her mind cried out in joy.

Isaac's lips had captured hers before she could think what to say, and then he moaned into her mouth as his thrusts culminated in wild heavy jerks.

And then it was over. At least, over for Isaac, as far as Katarina could tell. She could barely tell where she was in the haze of pleasure and gratification still rippling through her body. Isaac had fallen into her arms, and she held him, held him close.

The only man she would ever love.

Their breathing, quick and shallow, matched perfectly. Katarina had never felt so close to anyone in her life. The intimacy of the act, not just the physical nature of it, left her shivering.

Isaac Emmett. A man who had known precisely what she wanted and given it to her freely, taking what appeared to be no demands in return.

Katarina stroked his hair. "Isaac," she whispered.

Isaac lifted his head and kissed her lightly. "Kat."

She smiled. "You are…you are everything to me."

It was only then that it struck her that though she had been open with him about her emptions, about how she felt about him—she had even told him that she loved him—Isaac had said almost nothing in return.

But did that matter? How could it when they had shared something so glorious?

"Kat," Isaac said gently, his breath still shallow, "Kat, you are everything to me. Everything. I will never be complete now without you by my side."

CHAPTER EIGHT

KATARINA WAS USUALLY rather particular about where she slept. When her mother, Leonora, had informed her that Maria would be moving into her bedchamber over the festive period to ensure there was enough space for all the Fitzroy cousins, Katarina had not been pleased.

"My bedchamber is a sacred space," she had announced dramatically at luncheon at the time. "And it is outrageous that you are even considering betraying that sacredness!"

And yet, as daylight started to meander through her closed eyelids, and Katarina started to move uncomfortably from sleep to awake, she could not help but notice that her bed was far less comfortable than she remembered.

Why, they had never spent money to improve the mattress, but surely it was not this scratchy! And the smell—why, it smelled just like the cowshed!

Katarina opened her eyes. She was lying on her side, and absolutely everything in her vision was hay. Actual hay.

It took a moment, but then she remembered what had occurred the night before, and a wide smile crept over her face.

"Christ alive, Kat, you are not wearing any undershifts!"

"I know."

"But how did you—"

"I just knew,"

She was warm, and the reason for that warmth was immediately apparent. As Katarina glanced down, she saw an arm over her waist, holding her tight. An arm she recognized.

Turning her head ever so slightly, Katarina saw Isaac nestled up against her, and her heart sang.

Isaac Emmett. Well, she had been concerned he may not consider her as someone worthy of a future, and look what had happened. She had asked for what she wanted, and by goodness, she had got it.

"Tell me if you want more."

"More? More, more, more!"

Katarina swallowed and tried to remind herself that no one knew what they had shared together. Isaac was not the sort of man to go crowing about it. They would simply have to pretend that their wedding night was the first time that they had enjoyed such pleasures.

The real question was, how would they ever be able to keep their hands off each between now and the wedding?

Katarina sighed happily. Small details they would be sure to work out. For a start, Isaac would have to give his notice to Luke. Would Luke be difficult about it, make the man work his notice?

Surely not, Katarina decided. Why, when she had mentioned Isaac's name yesterday evening at the ball, Luke had not suggested she was wild for caring about him, had he?

"Well, I think there are probably a few things that he needs to talk to you about before conversation of the future can begin. If you do not mind me being so bold, Kitty."

Now she came to think about it, it was a rather strange thing to say. But then Luke was a teasing sort of fellow, Katarina knew. It was a most irritating habit, and his poor wife in the future would have to put up with much, whomever she ended up being.

Whereas she…she had the most perfect husband.

Katarina attempted to move around very slowly to look at Isaac, but the gentle movement and the growing dawn was enough to wake him.

Eyes scrunched up against the light, Isaac sighed heavily and shifted, pulling Katarina with him as he moved to lie on his back.

He chuckled. "Still here?"

"Nowhere else I would rather be," said Katarina happily, resting her head on his chest and listening to the slow, steady beat of his heart.

Reliable, like Isaac was. There was so much she loved about him, and at the same time, so much for her to discover. Was any other future bride as fortunate? Katarina could not believe so. None of them were betrothed to Isaac Emmett.

"I would have thought you would creep back to the house to your own bed," Isaac said sleepily.

Katarina chuckled, her hand around his chest. "No, I wanted to stay right here with you."

"You probably would have got a much better night's sleep."

Isaac's voice was quiet, slow. His eyes were still shut. Katarina tried not to laugh. It appeared her future husband was not particularly a morning person. Well, that would be interesting. She was always bright in the morning, eager to enter the day. It must have been difficult for Isaac, being a servant and not liking the morning.

A challenge he would never have to worry about when they were married. Katarina sighed happily. They would find a small house somewhere in a town, some place where life happened. They would have neighbors, favorite walks. She would have her dowry. Perhaps they could open a little shop.

"I slept perfectly well, actually," she said softly. "And you seem to have snored perfectly well without a bed beneath you."

Isaac laughed at that, his eyes finally opening. "I do not snore!"

"Worse than the cows," said Katarina with a grin. "I shall have to train that out of you, it will be most distressing."

"I am not sure anyone can be trained out of snoring, Kat," said Isaac. "Not in three days, anyway!"

Katarina frowned. Three days? What on earth did he mean by

that? "Why would you only give me three days to achieve such a monumental task?"

"Well, you're going to find it a bit of a challenge to train me when you're here at Chalcroft, and I'm back at Kingsley Hall."

Katarina relaxed. Well, that made sense. Luke and Isaac would have to return home at some point, and it was only right that she was married from Chalcroft. If they were swift, they may be able to have the wedding prepared before Easter. A Lenten wedding would be so elegant.

"Oh, I see what you mean," she said softly, closing her eyes and breathing in his musky scent. "I suppose I shall have to pick up my training when you return."

"Whenever that will be."

"Oh, I suppose we can get everything organized pretty swiftly," said Katarina quietly. "I would not want too much fuss after all, though Olivia may be a little put out. Being the eldest, I mean."

Somehow, even with her eyes closed, Katarina could tell something was wrong. There was a stiffness in Isaac that had not been there before.

There was some small problem, it appeared. Well, she thought sleepily, nothing that could not be resolved, one way or another. Nothing was going to stand in their way of happiness. Not a thing.

"Why would Olivia be put out?" Isaac said slowly. "And what are we organizing?"

Katarina smiled as she lifted her head to look into his eyes. Handsome eyes. And a mouth she wished to kiss.

She leaned forward, her desire for him overriding any thoughts, but Isaac turned away.

"What are we organizing?" he repeated.

Katarina smiled. "Why, the wedding, of course. I think Olivia always believed she would be wed first—she is the oldest, of course—but 'tis hardly my fault I have found the man I loved before she has. Found her own, I mean."

Isaac sat up rather hastily. "Wedding?"

It had been such a rush that Katarina had fallen to the hay, but it was a soft landing. She sat up, wondering whether her hair was as disheveled as Isaac's was. She would need to attempt to pull the straw from her hair before anyone saw her that morning. Perhaps a milk-maid could assist her.

"Yes, wedding," Katarina said, mind hardly on her words.

Isaac looked astonished, and when he spoke, it was in slow and careful tones. "Kat...Katarina, what did I say last night that gave you any indication that this...this escapade would end in a wedding?"

Katarina's heart stopped. Her skin chilled, her stomach lurched painfully, and for some awful reason, her heart did not seem able to beat.

"Kat...Katarina, what did I say last night that gave you any indication that this...this escapade would end in a wedding?"

She could not have heard him correctly. Of course there was going to be a wedding—how else would they become husband and wife? Had it not been clear—had *she* not been clear that she loved him, wanted him, wanted to be by his side forever?

"You—you said..." Katarina swallowed, trying to force her lungs to work. She needed more breath, but her heart was now lurching in awkward beats that was most upsetting.

Dread was entering her soul. Had she...had she made one of the biggest mistakes of her life?

"You said you wanted me by your side," she managed to say.

Isaac's eyes were wide, his face pale. "But I did not—dear God, Kat, a man can wish for a thing without expecting to get it!"

"But you can, you can have me," Katarina said quickly. "Do you not see, I want to marry you!"

"Wanting and getting are two very different things, Kat, and if you had lived the life I had, you would know that," said Isaac, rising to his feet hastily.

Katarina hardly knew what to say. It was so opposite to what she had expected that she could barely take in his words.

Wanting and getting were different things? Yes, to be sure, semantically; but in this situation, was not their path clear? Katarina could not understand why he appeared to be so astonished by her words. Had he not given himself to her—had he not taken her, all of her?

"I do not understand," she said quietly, still seated in the hay. "Do…do you not want to marry me?"

"Of course I want to marry you!" exploded Isaac. "But it's not that simple!"

"You don't have to shout at me," said Katarina, pain in every syllable. "I have done nothing wrong, and neither have you. We…we are talking of how we love each other."

Isaac brushed a hand madly through his hair, looking all around the cowshed, anywhere but at her.

And then he sighed. "You are right. I apologize, I…I should not have shouted. But I do not think you quite understand what is happening here, Kat."

Kat. Katarina's spirits lifted somewhat. She was still Kat. That had to mean something. Didn't it?

"I think I do know what is happening," she said, getting to her feet. "I think I know perfectly. You are worried about the future."

"I am worried about right now!" Isaac said with a dry laugh. "Kat…Kat, you are a Fitzroy. A lady with certain expectations about the life you want to life, about the future that you want for yourself."

"But I don't want Chalcroft!" Katarina had to make him understand, even as her ears throbbed with her own pulse. "You think I want to live in a large manor, in the middle of nowhere, and not see anyone? A small house in a town would suit us perfectly; drawing room, smoking room, breakfast room, a few bedchambers for guests—"

She was interrupted by Isaac's laughter. "Kat, do you hear yourself? Do you know what I own in the whole world?"

Katarina hesitated. She had never known much about the Chalcroft servants, not that she would own it. True, she had conversations with the milkmaids, considered herself friendly with them, but it was only in this moment that she realized she knew very little about them. About that different kind of life.

"No," she said softly. "No, I don't."

Isaac thrust his hand into his pocket and brought out something, then opened his palm toward her. On it lay three shillings.

"That is all," he said in a low voice. "That is all I have to offer you, Kat, offer a Fitzroy! You think your father would appreciate his child being taken away to—to where? To work at Kingsley Hall? Would you be happy as the wife to a servant in the home of your friend?"

Katarina swallowed. "I have my dowry—we could buy a small house, and—"

"And how long would that last?" Isaac interrupted. "I have nothing to offer you."

"You have yourself," said Katarina warmly, stepping toward him.

Oh, if only she could make him see himself as she saw him: a tower of strength, a kind and benevolent man, one who with hard work and industry could surely do anything, anything he put his mind do.

"You are more than enough for me, for any woman who had the good sense and fortune to attract your affections," Katarina said, reaching Isaac and taking the shillings from his hand. "Shillings…shillings can be gained, earned, found, inherited. But a good man—a man like yourself is something a wise person would never pass up the chance to have. For…for richer, for poorer."

Her eyes met his, and she saw the pain within them. He wanted to offer her everything, she could see that, but then why could he not see that everything was not what she wanted?

"And you think you could be happy without all the trimmings a Chalcroft Christmas has to offer?" Isaac's words cut through her thoughts, forcing her to look directly into his eyes. "Because this isn't just something that you would have to learn to live with for a few days or a week, Kat. This would be forever.

How can I compete with Chalcroft?"

Why couldn't he see that Chalcroft was not perfect? Katarina could think of nothing to say but, "You have already competed with Chalcroft, and look—you won!"

She spread her arms out wide. Straw fell from her hair, the perfect hair that she had created for the ball—a ball she had barely attended.

"My sisters, cousins, parents, all their friends, they stayed in Chalcroft for the ball," Katarina said quietly, not looking away from him. "That was what they wanted. I...I came here. To find you. *You* are what I want."

For a moment, she was certain he finally understood her; that he would smile, pull her into his arms, and kiss away the confusion and pain; would tell her that she was right. That everything was going to be alright.

But he did not. Isaac just stood there, staring at her.

"And you are what I want," he said quietly. "But I just...I do not see how this will work, Kat. I am sorry."

Katarina swallowed, forcing back the tears that threatened to fall. She was not going to cry.

"I...I can't explain to you how wrong I think you are," Katarina said helplessly.

Isaac smiled wryly. "I could say the same to you. Go on. They'll be looking for you, at the house. That's...that's where you belong."

Katarina glanced over her shoulder at the towering rooftops of Chalcroft. She had never felt less like she belonged there, but some of what Isaac said she could not deny. They would be looking for her. It would be too much to hope that her absence had continued to go unnoticed.

"This conversation is not over," she said, turning on her heels with a sudden determination. "I am going up to the house, yes, but to tell my father everything. I am sure he will—"

"Kat, no!"

But Isaac's words did not prevent Katarina stepping forward, her fingers finding the latch to the cowshed as she forced open the door.

Bright dazzling sunlight struck her face, and Katarina raised her hand to shield her eyes. It had been pitch black when she had last walked out here, desperate to find Isaac, to make him understand how she felt about him.

Now, after all they had shared, Katarina was not entirely sure whether he did yet. He still held onto this strange idea that she needed to be protected, to be cared for with money, rather than love.

Was that all it came down to for men, she thought irritably as she walked forward across the stable yard toward the drive at the front of Chalcroft. Was that all men could conceive of? Money and income and wealth? She had thought Isaac different.

"Katarina!"

He was striding behind her, she could hear his footsteps, but she did not halt her steps. She meant it. It was time her Papa knew precisely how she felt about Isaac Emmett, even if neither man was ready for it.

"Katarina Fitzroy!"

It was not Isaac's voice that called out this time, but her mother. Katarina looked up, still blinking in the sunlight, to see a rather intimidating sight.

Fitzroys. All of them—at least, what felt like all of them. Katarina swallowed as her family poured down the front steps of Chalcroft toward her, each of them with various expressions of fear and concern on their faces.

Ah. So, her absence had been noted, then. Damn, she should have thought to say something to Maria, something about enjoying the ball so much that she would stay up all night and break her fast with the servants.

That would have been the smart thing to do, Katarina could see now. Her mother was frowning, her cousins curious, and her father led the pack of them with a strange expression on his face.

Was it…fear?

"Katarina Fitzroy, what have you done! We had no idea where you were!" her Papa said as the Fitzroy gaggle met Katarina, moving into a semi-circle around her. "Where on earth have you been?"

"Your bed wasn't slept in," said Maria, almost apologetically. "I was worried that—"

"Is that straw in your hair?" asked Jemima, not waiting for her younger cousin to finish. "You haven't slept in a stable, have you?"

"Very Christmassy," said Harmony with a wry smile. "And Jemima, you shouldn't be out here in the cold, not in your condition. Goodness, Katarina, you did give us a fright, though. Why on earth did you sleep out there?"

Jemima's condition? What on earth did that mean?

But Katarina could not think about Jemima or any of her cousins or sisters. She had to think about herself.

She took a deep breath. There would be no going back from this, she knew. Once she said these words, the scandal would be out. There would be no holding it back. She would have to trust her family, all the Fitzroys, that they would keep it in the family.

But then boldness rose in her heart, and her shoulders straightened. What did it matter if the whole world knew? She would marry Isaac Emmett either way and be proud to be his wife. This Christmas, the best gift she could receive would be him. All of him.

"I," she began.

"Kat," came a low, warning voice behind her.

Katarina turned to see Isaac, holding up a hand as though that could stop her. She smiled, and he smiled back. She reached out her hand, and he hesitated before taking it.

"Kat?" repeated her father with a suspicious expression. "That is a rather intimate name to be calling my daughter, young man."

"It is, sir," said Isaac quietly. "And I would not do so unless I had your daughter's permission."

Katarina's heart swelled. Everything was going to be fine. All she had to do was explain a few little things to her Papa, and then—

"That is straw in your hair," said Lucy in a sharp tone. "Did you take a tumble in the hay?"

Katarina smiled weakly. "In…in a manner of speaking."

She squeezed Isaac's hand, and he immediately squeezed hers back. They stood together, shoulder to shoulder, ready to face the scorn of her family.

William Fitzroy let out a bark of laughter. "If you think I will permit you to touch my daughter for one minute longer, you cad—"

"I am sure there is a perfectly reasonable explanation," said Esther soothingly.

"Reasonable explanation, be damned!" exploded Katarina's father. "Dear God, you mean to say—tumble in the hay?"

Katarina flushed, but did not drop her gaze, nor relinquish Isaac's hand. She would not give him up, no matter what her father said. No matter what anyone said. She loved him.

"Yes," she said calmly.

Leonora's hand leapt to her chest, and Joy muttered a curse that Katarina had never heard before. Jemima looked to her husband swiftly, and Isabella's eyes were wide, her mouth open.

Katarina swallowed. "I think Papa, Isaac, and I need to discuss—"

"There is absolutely nothing to discuss!" Her Papa drew up to his full height, and glared not at his daughter, but at the man holding her hand. "I will have satisfaction, sir!"

CHAPTER NINE

"N O—NO ONE IS going to duel anyone!" Katarina stepped between her father and her lover, arms outstretched, absolutely determined to prevent anything so dramatic as a duel.

Her father's words were echoing in her mind.

"There is absolutely nothing to discuss! I will have satisfaction, sir!"

Never had it entered her mind that her father could take the news in such a way—it was barbaric! Surely no grown man, no man with any feeling, could consider it appropriate to demand satisfaction from the man she loved.

Katarina glanced at Isaac, whose blood was clearly up by the look of fury on his face, and then at her father, whose hands had clenched into fists by his side.

This had been a mistake. She should not have been so bold, so direct in her explanation of what had happened. She should have waited, encouraged everyone else to return to the house, then calmly explained to her Papa that she was in love with Isaac.

Perhaps if she had managed to do that, then her father and her lover would not now be threatening to kill each other.

As if that wasn't bad enough, Katarina saw from the corner of her eye that the milk-maids, expecting to enter the cowshed to carry out their morning milking, were standing a little way back, but evidently watching.

Heat flushed her cheeks, and Katarina wished she had

thought about this for more than a moment. That was the trouble with passion, she thought. It had rather got her into a few scrapes, now she came to think about it.

"Satisfaction?" repeated Leonora. Katarina's mother looked absolutely astonished. "Not at your age, William, surely!"

"I would be honored to step into your place if needed, sir," said Jemima's husband stiffly.

With a sinking heart, it was only then that Katarina remembered that Hugh, Jemima's husband, was a trained soldier. Isaac would be no match for a man who knew his way so easily around a weapon—she doubted whether Isaac had ever held a gun in his life.

"Absolutely not," said Jemima firmly. "Hugh, you know you should not risk it, risk leaving us—"

"That will not be necessary," Katarina said sharply. "No one is going to—"

"You cannot just expect us to accept this, Katarina," her father said sternly. "You must have known when this brigand—"

"I am no such thing," said Isaac hotly.

"Please, Papa," said Katarina desperately. "The maids, they should be milking."

Her father looked around and saw the eight maids standing there, who suddenly all had something rather interesting to inspect on their hands, their gowns, or in the sky.

"Be off with you," he called over to them, not unkindly. "Nothing to see here."

Nothing to see here, thought Katarina sardonically. She had never considered her father the king of understatement before, but she did now.

Nothing to see, nothing to see—only the master threatening a coachman with murder for bedding his thirdborn daughter.

Nothing other than that...

"You should all go inside," said Katarina hastily, hoping that the removal of the milk-maids would encourage the rest of the Fitzroy family to similarly dissipate. "My father and Isaac and I—"

"There is no 'Isaac and I,'" growled her Papa, glaring at the man standing behind Katarina. "Never was, not now, and never will be."

"I want to be Katarina Emmett," Katarina said passionately, turning to her father. "It is a solid enough name, why should I not leave Fitzroy for it?"

"We will talk about this later," he hissed.

"Papa—"

"Do not get in the way, Kitty," hissed Isabella, her eyes wide as she stared at Isaac, clearly unfriendly. "Do you not see what you have done? You have ruined yourself, and us, too, if words gets out!"

"Word will not get out," Katarina said hastily. "I trust everyone here. I do not believe—"

"And the milkmaids?" shot back Maria in a rare outburst in public. "Good God, Kitty, you have not just ended your chances for a good match, but that of our own! Do you think anyone would wish to—"

"At least Olivia is not here to hear such news," Leonora muttered as Katarina attempted to control her temper.

It was most provoking. She had done naught wrong, as far as she could see. True, she probably should not have allowed herself to be bedded by Isaac until the formalities were concluded, and yes, now she came to think about it, it was rather awkward that he had almost refused to marry her, but still...

"We should leave," murmured Joy to her younger sister Harmony, who nodded. "Uncle William, we will just go inside while you discuss this with Mr.—"

"There is no need for discussion!" shouted William, glaring at his daughter. Katarina glared back. "My daughter knows precisely what she has done, and this boy, I do not give him the honor of being called a man, will pay for it!"

"Yes, if you do not mind going inside, Joy," Katarina said hastily. "And Esther, Lucy, Jemima, you can all go—"

"Not if Mr. Fitzroy requires my services," said Hugh, rolling up his sleeves and glaring at Isaac. "A man insults a Fitzroy, he insults us all."

Katarina sighed as her family fell into bickering as to who should stay outside and give Isaac what was coming to him, and who should go inside to prevent greater embarrassment.

It was all so…so infuriating. So unnecessary. Why was it that men reached more often for their fists than a handshake? Why was it so important to men that they demonstrated their prowess for all to see, rather than attempted to discuss this rationally, like adults?

Katarina tried to think, but her mind was whirling with thoughts and ideas she could not entirely control. She wanted to reason with her family; she wanted to calm her mother; she wanted to kiss Isaac.

She would have to wait before indulging in that last one.

If she was not able to convince her parents that Isaac was not only a good man, but a good enough man to marry their daughter, then she may find kissing Isaac a far more difficult task than she initially hoped.

"But you simply cannot fight, William, you are too…mature," her mother, Leonora, was saying.

Katarina could have told her mother immediately that that was not the right tack to take. Her father swelled up with indignation at the suggestion that his age may have a negative bearing on the whole thing, and immediately raised his voice, as though by shouting louder, his points were somehow more impressive.

"I think I am far more able to deal with this matter than you think, Leonora!" he bellowed. "When I had our daughters, I always said—"

"You had our daughters?" Katarina's mama raised an eyebrow.

William hesitated, a little abashed. "Well. You know what I mean. When *we* had them…"

Their discussion continued.

Katarina turned with wide eyes to Isaac. "Do something."

"What would you have me do?" murmured Isaac, his face serious and his gaze not flinching from hers. "You did not think this through, Kat, and you should…you should have waited. We could have discussed this the two of us, understood precisely what we wanted to say, and—"

A spark of hope flickered in Katarina's heart. "Then you…you still want to marry me?"

Isaac grinned. "More than anything—but that does not mean it is the best thing for you, Kat. I hope you can see that. I want what is best for you, and that may not be me."

But Katarina did not heed his words—not all of them, at least. He wanted to marry her. Her! Isaac Emmett would be her husband, and they would be happy together, for what else could they be when two people who loved each other were permitted to be together?

Well. They were not quite there yet. From what Katarina could see, her parents were no closer to agreeing that she could marry Isaac than they were agreeing to sell Chalcroft.

"—pistols in the gun room," her father was saying to Hugh in an undertone. "If you could retrieve—"

"No one is going to need pistols!" Katarina interrupted, her stomach lurching.

Pistols…unreliable at the best of times, and her father had not shot with a pistol for years. Isaac, surely, had never touched one in his life.

She was not going to lose the two men she loved over a squabble.

"Papa, this is silly," Katarina tried to say. "I do not want you to fight each other!"

"But you give me no choice!" Her Papa looked physically pained as he glared over her shoulder at Isaac. "That—that cad has besmirched you, Kitty, and he must pay for it!"

Katarina looked around wildly. Olivia was the only sister who perhaps would be on her side, would be able to persuade their father to calm down—but she was nowhere to be seen. Where on earth was she?

"Well, you cannot fight Isaac if he does not fight you," Katarina said passionately. "And he won't, so you can just go inside and—"

"I accept your challenge, sir, by the Viscount Braedon's rules, which as I am given to understand have not changed since I left Oxford. May I select a second?"

Katarina froze. No. She could not have heard those words. It was not possible. It had sounded, though her ears must surely be paying tricks on her...it sounded as though those words came from behind her, and the only person standing behind her was...Isaac.

She whirled around. Isaac was staring imperiously at her father, his whole demeanor altered. His back was straighter, his eyes sharper, and he was holding himself stiffly, like...like a gentleman who had himself been dishonored.

But she could not have heard that correctly. Isaac would not have accepted the challenge. He would surely know that it would be more than his life was worth to take on a gentleman like her father at a gentleman's game.

"I accept your challenge, sir, by the Viscount Braedon's rules, which as I am given to understand have not changed since I left Oxford. May I select a second?"

The words echoed in her head as they echoed around the drive, and Katarina saw she was not the only one who was staring, transfixed, at Isaac.

But now she had a moment to think about them, Katarina realized that there was far more in those words than a mere acceptance.

The Viscount Braedon's rules—how did Isaac know about them? A mere coachman could not be expected to know the particular rules and regulations of dueling and challenges, could he? Unless, Katarina thought wildly, unless Luke had been drawn into a challenge or two in his time, only as a second or a witness of course, and Isaac—who would have driven him to the agreed dueling locations—had picked up the language?

But no. As Katarina stared at his tightened jaw and determined air, she could see quite plainly that he understood the rules perfectly. As though he had been taught them.

"Since you left Oxford," repeated Jemima. "What do you mean, since you left Oxford?"

Katarina swallowed. The more she looked at Isaac, the more she was starting to wonder that herself.

Isaac Emmett. He was a tall man, a handsome man, a charming one, and in the last few days of heady courtship, she had not asked questions that perhaps she should have done.

How was a coachman so witty, so quick? How did he know so much about the type of life she led—how was he so sure their lives were totally separate?

And now she came to think about it, there were large gaps in her knowledge about him, too, that he already knew about her. Who were his family? What profession had his father been, that they had argued so terribly and broken apart for so long?

Katarina swallowed. Her throat was dry. Just as she thought she had found someone to know and love and trust, there were questions forming in her mind about just how well she could depend on someone she had only met a week ago.

Isaac Emmett was still the man she loved. She knew that. Katarina's affections for him were unchanged, and if he asked for her hand this instant she would, with her Papa's blessing, marry him tomorrow.

But what sort of man was she marrying? Servant—or gentleman?

"Explain yourself, boy," snapped her father. "What is all this?"

Isaac stepped around Katarina and approached her father.

"Isaac—no, wait—"

"My name is Isaac Arthur Emmett Pembroke," Isaac said in a clear, ringing voice, "and I am the fourth son of the Duke of Pembroke."

There were no gasps; there was no sound at all. For a moment, Katarina was concerned her hearing had disappeared altogether.

The entire Fitzroy family, still without Olivia and Luke, which Katarina could not understand, were staring at him. Their gazes seemed to fix him in place, for Isaac made no movement to step forward, though he did continue to speak in a low voice. He did not need to speak any louder; he had their complete attention.

"My father and I argued, several years ago, about the mistreatment of my sister," Isaac was saying quietly. "She wished to wed someone very dear to her and was forbidden from doing so because it was believed his nobility was in question."

"But—but…Duke of Pembroke?" said William quietly.

Isaac nodded. "I am, I suppose, Viscount, Lord Pembroke. But I have not gone by that name for many years. I have found work, honest work where I can, and refused to touch the inheritance my father laid aside for me."

Isaac Arthur Emmett Pembroke…fourth son of the Duke of Pembroke…inheritance…

Words swam around Katarina's mind, but she was unable to focus on any single one of them for more than a moment.

It did not make sense. It could not be true—it was a jest, a trick. A way for Isaac to avoid hurting her father, that must be it.

But as Katarina looked up at the man by her side, the man who had taken her hand in his as he spoke, she saw the truth in him.

He was a duke's son. There was an arrogance, a power there which she had seen before and been attracted to, but…perhaps because it had felt so unusual to find it in a servant. The way he had spoken to her, the haughtiness of his tone—the jesting he made at her expense.

The way he called her Kat.

It all made sense now. How could she not have seen it before? She had known Isaac was not like any other servant she had ever encountered before, and there was a reason for that.

Because he had never been destined for a life in the stables. He was a gentleman, a gentleman moreover with not gentry, but noble blood in his veins.

He was destined for greatness, for a mansion far more impressive than Chalcroft. Diamonds and riches would be poured into his wife's lap.

And Katarina saw, all too clearly, that she had been tricked. That the simple life, the small house in a town where they could open a little shop and keep themselves that way…that was all over.

Marriage to Isaac Arthur Emmett Pembroke would make her a lady. Would mean she would need to go to London for the Season, dress up in fancy silks, be seen in all the right places, be sure to befriend some and snub others.

That was not the life she had expected. Had wanted.

"Fourth son of a duke, you say?" Her Papa, on the other hand, was experiencing quite a different dilemma. "Well, that is quite different. That puts an entirely new light on the matter, do not you think, Leonora?"

"Quite," said her mother faintly. She dropped into an awkward curtsey, and then straightened up and tried to whisper in her husband's ear. "Perhaps…a little hasty…"

"Yes, a little too hasty, that was precisely what I was going to say," said William quickly. "I may have been hasty, boy—sir—my lord, I mean—and I am sure if we sit down, perhaps over a little brandy, never too early on Christmas Day…"

Katarina's heart sank. It was all going wrong.

When her father had believed Isaac to be no more than a coachman, a driver, a servant, he had been outraged at the mere possibility of him even touching her.

The idea that Katarina had given herself to him…

Well, it had led to shouts and much upset and the suggestion of a duel.

But now her father knew Isaac to be not only a man of good breeding and good blood, but with a title and some sort of inheritance to boot, everything was different. Her mother was still attempting to curtsey, and her cousins had scarlet cheeks as they considered how the fourth son of a duke had been spoken to.

"Here you go, sir," said Hugh panting, holding out a pair of pistols. "I found them in the gun room, right where you said they would—"

"We don't need those, not anymore," said her Papa eagerly, clapping a hand around Hugh's shoulders. "Rotherham, let me introduce you to—if I may, of course, my lord—to Isaac Pembroke, fourth son of the Duke of Pembroke."

Hugh's eyes widened. Evidently, he had been in the house looking for the pistols when the revelation had been made, and Katarina saw the same sudden shock on his face that all her family had displayed.

Why, Isabella was staring as though she had never seen a gentleman before in her life, and Maria—Maria, Katarina saw with a wry grin, had disappeared.

It was all so sickening. The hypocrisy of it all, Katarina could hardly bear it. Why must her father make such a spectacle of himself? Why must he make it so obvious that he was only now interested in having Isaac as a son-in-law because he would give her the Pembroke name?

For it was not Emmett that she was leaving the Fitzroy name for, she knew that now. It was Pembroke and all the responsibilities that came with it.

Katarina swallowed. Her mouth was still dry, her throat sore, and suddenly the words she was thinking but had vowed she would not say tumbled out from her lips.

"You…you lied to me."

The Fitzroy family went quiet, their babbling ceasing. Even her father stopped trying to make overtures of forgiveness and reconciliation.

Katarina dropped Isaac's hand and took a small step away from him as he turned to look at him, his face stricken.

"Kat, it wasn't like that—"

"You all go back to the house and take his lordship with you," Katarina mumbled. "I…I need to be alone."

Without waiting to hear his apologies, his explanations, or the hurried demands of her father that she would now marry the man, Katarina turned and started to walk away.

CHAPTER TEN

WORDS FADED BEHIND Katarina as she walked away, unheeding them.

"—needs some time to think, let's go back to the house—"

"—calm down once she's had a few moments to think—"

"No, leave her be, Isabella, we'll not go after her. When Kitty's ready, she'll come back to Chalcroft."

Back to Chalcroft, Katarina thought bitterly as she strode forward, not entirely sure where she was going but certain in the knowledge that she had to get away from here, no matter the cost.

Back to Chalcroft? Back to be laughed at by her sisters for accidentally falling in love with a duke's son. For thinking he was a mere servant, and being willing to stand by him, no matter what his status.

Red-hot anger mingled with shame, shot through her veins, and made her fury grow as Katarina marched forward with no thought where she was going.

How could she have been so stupid? Why had she not seen the signs, so numerous now, she could hardly believe she had not asked at the time. He had called Luke by his first name, for goodness's sake! He was evidently on equal enough terms with Lord Kingsley that Isaac felt comfortable enough calling him by his first name!

And did that mean, Katarina thought with a lurch of her stomach, that Luke knew the whole truth? What was it that he said last night?

"Well, I think there are probably a few things that he needs to talk to you about before conversation of the future can begin. If you do not mind me being so bold, Kitty."

Tears threatened to fall as Katarina brushed them aside. He had known all along, and had not thought to tell her the truth, but instead had kept it hidden. Kept laughing at her.

Perhaps that was where he and Olivia were now, laughing at her. They evidently thought her a fool if she was unable to discern that a man posing as a servant was not what he said he was.

Whether Katarina had intended it or not, her feet had taken her back to the cowshed. She pulled open the door, stepped in, and was welcomed with the warm, comforting cowness of the air.

"Miss Katarina, we did not mean to intrude—Miss Katarina!"

Katarina blinked. Of course. Just because it was Christmas Day, that did not mean that the cows did not need milking. Eight maids were milking in steady streams, milk pouring into the buckets beneath them.

One of the maids, Molly, was closest to her. "You look mighty upset, Miss Katarina, if you do not mind me saying so."

Katarina took a deep breath but had no idea what she could possibly say. How could she? She had no wish for even more people to know of her foolishness.

It was so…so unfair. She had thought she had found someone with whom she could truly be herself, yet the whole time, Isaac had been lying.

She had been honest with him when she had spoken of her desire to be with him no matter his status or lack of wealth, but Isaac had known all along, hadn't he, that he was a gentleman of far greater birth than she.

"I have found work, honest work, where I can, and refused to touch

the inheritance my father laid aside for me."

He had probably been laughing at her the entire time, Katarina thought dully. *He took my innocence, for he knew that there would be no repercussions for a duke's son. That was all. If he truly loved me, would he not be here, chasing after me, instead of—*

"Kat!"

Katarina did not turn, though she knew the sound of that voice well enough. Isaac. He had come after her.

It did not lessen the shame she felt. If anything, it merely increased it. The last thing Katarina wanted was another discussion about how entirely taken in she had been, how easily she had been fooled.

Especially not with the milkmaids here.

Color tinged her cheeks, and she looked desperately at Molly without saying a word.

There must be something about womanhood, Katarina thought later, for though she had said nothing, Molly seemed to understand exactly what she needed. Privacy.

She and Isaac would have one final conversation, one last opportunity for him to explain himself, and then Katarina could return to Chalcroft and the life she should have known she would never be able to escape.

And that would be that. Luke would leave with Isaac, and he could go and be a servant, or a duke, or whatever it was that he wanted. And she would never see him again.

Katarina swallowed. Never again.

"Come on, girls," said Molly cheerfully. "Let's take the cows out, 'tis a beautiful morning, and they would appreciate the sunshine. Come on now."

She brooked no argument, and within a minute, Katarina and Isaac were left alone in the cowshed.

Katarina's heart ached. This was all she had wanted when she had first met Isaac, the chance to be alone with him. To talk with him. To kiss him, for she had seen the desire in his eyes and known it was returned.

But so much had happened since then. They had made love, and he had betrayed her.

"You…you do not seem very happy, Kat."

Katarina closed her eyes, took a deep breath, then opened them as she faced him.

Isaac stood there, handsome as ever, which was most infuriating, a wry smile on his face. He seemed utterly relaxed, his shoulders loose, a hand in his pocket.

Rage sparked in Katarina's heart. Isaac appeared to be utterly at peace with the whole thing, uncaring that he had just imploded Katarina's world. Did he not care? Did he have no empathetic bone in his body?

"I am not happy," she said stiffly. "You lied to me. You—you seduced me under false pretenses."

"I hardly think hiding my birth was false pretenses," Isaac said quietly as he took a step toward her, but he halted as she glared at him. "Kat—"

"Do not call me that," said Katarina, her heart breaking.

If only she had never found out; if only they had eloped, without seeing her family. Then perhaps he would have told her in his own time, when they were alone, when she had the time to take it all in.

As it was…

"Why not?"

"Because only someone who truly knows me, and I truly know in return, should be allowed to give me pet names," said Katarina, swallowing down her desperate need to cry. "And I do not know you, do I, Isaac? Or should that be *my lord*?"

Isaac winched. "Come on, Kat, you know I don't care for that sort of thing."

"Do I?" challenged Katarina, a little more fire in her voice. "I thought you were a servant, Isaac, you said that you had argued with and broken with your father—"

"That is true," he interrupted with a rueful smile. "I never actually told you a lie. We are from different worlds, you and I, though…perhaps not the two you thought."

Katarina stared at him helplessly. How could she make him understand? Why was she not able to make him see just how infuriating it was that he had kept such a monumental truth from her?

Taking a deep breath, she sighed heavily. "Isaac, I do not think I can explain how…how betrayed I feel."

"But—"

"No, let me finish," Katarina said, raising a hand.

Isaac bit his lip, as though the words he desperately wanted to say were almost about to spill from his mouth, but nodded.

Katarina hesitated, trying to collect her thoughts. If this was the one opportunity she had to explain to Isaac just how she felt, how lost, how alone, then she wanted to do it justice.

If she could.

"I love you," she said simply. "But the man I fell in love with was a man who had not known the comforts and luxuries of a Chalcroft at Christmas. A man who did not find value in titles nor wealth nor finery. A man who would be happy with me, and nothing else, and I had been honest with you, and…"

Katarina's voice trailed away. No, it was not possible. She could not explain it.

But somehow, her lack of words had a greater impact on Isaac than any elegant soliloquy could have. There was a frown across his forehead now, a pain in his eyes that had not been there before.

"I had not considered it in such a way," Isaac said quietly. "I am sorry, Kat."

She nodded. "I know. But you must see, or at least I hope you can, how strange this all is to me. I mean, you are the son of a duke!"

"A man no greater than your father, and in my opinion, far less," said Isaac with a hint of darkness in his voice.

Katarina could not help herself. She took a step forward,

needing to be closer to him. "What do you mean? My father has no title, he is not even a baronet."

"Yet, he is a better man than my father ever could be," said Isaac with some feeling. "Your father understands the important things, that family, love, and friendship are more important than prestige, duty, and one's reputation."

Katarina raised an eyebrow. It all felt for a moment as though so much was held in the balance; her love for him was unchanging, but a part of her now wondered whether it could now lead to something truly wonderful…

"I am not so sure of that," she said quietly. "Both your father and mine became quite agitated, by the sound of it, at the thought of their daughter marrying someone beneath them."

Isaac chuckled. "I suppose you are right. But my sister was not permitted to marry a viscount, a lineage my father did not believe was suitably noble. Your father would have accepted me if he had known me a gentleman, I believe, regardless of my blood."

Katarina nodded mutely. It was all so strange. What she had been entirely sure of just hours ago was all in flux.

Isaac was not a servant. He was a lord. More, her father was seriously considering her marriage to him; she had seen it in the way his eyes had lit up when Isaac revealed his parentage.

"I wish I had told you sooner," said Isaac suddenly, and Katarina flushed. "When I knew I loved you. When you welcomed me into your arms. I should have told you everything then, made it clear to you just what kind of man you were accepting."

"Yes, you should," said Katarina bluntly.

But she felt no spark of joy when Isaac looked downcast at her words, and suddenly, all the pain she had felt was gone, melted away by his clear contrition.

Isaac had done naught but run from his own family and privilege, and was that not precisely what she had been considering by marrying him?

She had seen the possibility of a life without so many rules and restrictions, without pomp and circumstance, and she had leapt at it. Had not Isaac done precisely the same?

"So," Katarina said quietly. "You are a lord. A viscount."

Isaac looked up and grinned to see her slow smile. "Only officially. The fourth son of a duke doesn't usually get so much in the way of titles and wealth."

She could not help but smile. "I suppose not. You…you did make me feel a fool, Isaac."

Isaac's smile slipped slightly. "I know, but I was the fool not to tell you. Oh Kat, if only I had seen it the first moment I met you, but…you honestly think you and I could have run away on nothing, worked our way through the world?"

Hope was starting to bud in Katarina's heart. There was such an easy manner between her and Isaac, one she had noticed the moment they had first conversed. They were meant to be together. She just knew it. There was something deep inside that connected them—and not just because she had given him her heart and her innocence.

"We might have managed it," said Katarina, stepping forward.

Isaac met her halfway, his hands taking hers, his fingers entwining hers. "We would have struggled, and you know it."

"I know no such thing!" Katarina laughed, her heart soaring now. Touching Isaac, even this small touch of fingers, was enough to bring relief to her soul—and to start building that ache between her legs again. "I am sure there are plenty of things I can do to earn money—I know how to milk a cow, you know!"

Isaac captured her lips with his, and Katarina gave herself up to him, to the pleasure he gave, to the certainty she had that he was the man she wanted, she needed to be with.

Tingles of pleasure rippled through her body, the ache in her stomach growing, and Katarina released her fingers from his grip so that she could pull him closer.

The kiss deepened, until Katarina was unaware of all around them. They could have been in the ballroom at Chalcroft, or the center of Almack's, or a slightly smelly cowshed, but it would have made no difference to the ardor she felt.

When Isaac eventually broke the kiss, Katarina stayed in his arms and looked up at him with a wide smile.

"Well, well, Lord Pembroke," she said with a mischievous smile. "What happens next?"

"Well, you are no milkmaid," said Isaac with a laugh. "And I have rather tired of the coachman life. Luke is a terrible master, you know, no boxes on Christmas Day, and he snores like the devil in the back of my carriage."

Katarina giggled. "Well, I am not sure my dowry will support us entirely you know, so unless we both take up milking—"

"Did I or did I not say that I had an inheritance waiting for me?"

Katarina stopped laughing. There was a strange sort of earnestness in his face that she adored. A gentle affection for her twinned with a desperation to please.

"Inheritance," she repeated. "What do you mean, inheritance?"

Isaac shrugged, his hands meandering from her hips to her buttocks. "Nothing really to speak of."

"Isaac Arthur Emmett Pembroke!" said Katarina in a mock severe tone, stroking his cheek. "If that even is your true name! You tell me what your inheritance is this minute, or I shall—"

"Shall?" teased Isaac. "Shall?"

Katarina grinned. "I shall never kiss you again."

"Dear God, a genuine threat," he said with a sigh. "Fine, but you will not like it."

Katarina's heart sank. She was not entirely sure whether she could bear many more surprises this morning. She had woken up in the arms of a servant and now found herself standing in the arms of a duke's son. What could possibly come next?

"Why won't I like it?" she said suspiciously.

Isaac sighed dramatically. "I mean, 'tis a trifle."

"Isaac!"

"Fine!" he laughed, holding her close, so close Katarina could feel his heartbeat through his shirt. It was rapid, vibrant, longing. "I have an income of three thousand a year and a small place in Kent. Very small."

Katarina's mouth fell open. Three—three thousand a year? That was in excess of what her father's income was, from what she could make out, and he managed to support four daughters on it!

Three thousand a year?

"A small place in Kent," she repeated hoarsely.

Isaac kissed her. "Just a small manor. Part of a large village, full of people, a market town on the way to London. Packed with different people every week. And the manor? Six bedchambers, library, gun room, a little land," he said as he kissed down her neck. "A farm that needs taking in hand, now I come to think about it. I may need to hire a maid to do my milking."

"Isaac Emmett—Pembroke, are you in earnest?" Katarina could hardly believe it.

Everything she had wanted was about to offer itself to her. The man she loved, an income they could rely on, and a home where she could be herself. Where she could do nothing if she wished, or go to town if she wished…

Isaac was smiling down at her. "And now, Katarina Fitzroy, I am going to do what I should have done when I first met you."

Katarina raised an eyebrow. "And what is that—Isaac!"

She was certain her shriek would be heard in Chalcroft, it was so loud—but then, she had not expected to be suddenly tipped over, her feet losing all purchase on the hay, finding herself lying on her back.

Isaac joined her immediately, kissing her furiously as he covered her body with his, and the intensity of the pleasure he gave her immediately pushed all thoughts from Katarina's mind. She just wanted to be with him, be possessed by him, know the touch of his hand on her—

"Isaac!"

Isaac lifted his head from her breast, which he had been kissing through the thin silk. "What?"

Heat was rushing through Katarina, but it was not only excitement, but embarrassment. "Anyone could come in here, anyone could see!"

Isaac shook his head with a grin. "Oh, I don't think so."

Even in the midst of passion, Katarina felt a prickle of concern. "You don't?"

"Your father instructed me to speak with you for as long as it took to convince you to marry me," Isaac said with a wicked smile on his face, "and ordered no one to interrupt me."

Katarina laughed, pulling Isaac closer to her. He had thought of everything, her clever husband-to-be. Whether she was forced to milk cows or not, she would have precisely what she needed right here, in her arms, as long as she had Isaac.

"In that case, Isaac, love me. Love me hard."

With a growl, Isaac leaned forward and kissed her hard on the mouth while his fingers scrabbled to release his manhood from his breeches. Katarina could barely think, but she knew enough of what she wanted to move her skirts swiftly, welcoming Isaac to her the moment his manhood was free.

But that was not enough, it seemed. Katarina looked up as Isaac pulled off his boots, breeches entirely, and then his shirt.

Katarina gasped. He was magnificent. Seeing him there, entirely nude, was to see the man she knew she would love until the very end of her days.

"Now you," Isaac said in a jagged voice. "I must see you, Kat. I want to see you, all of you."

She did not need much encouragement. Her silk gown buttons flew off into all corners of the cowshed as Katarina ripped it off, not willing to wait for her impatient fingers to carefully unbutton each one. She had no undershift on, no other garments, so as she pushed her gown down to her feet and slipped it off, casting it aside onto the hay, she lay there entirely naked and unashamed.

What did she have to feel ashamed of? Katarina knew that she and Isaac would be married within two weeks—her father would not be so foolish as to avoid a special license.

Why not show herself to her future husband? They had shared almost everything already.

Isaac's eyes were wide. "Dear God, you are so…so beautiful."

Katarina said nothing but extended her hands to him.

Isaac needed no further invitation. She gasped as he pressed his warm body against hers; the intensity of the sensation was almost overwhelming, but was heightened by the way his hands touched her, teased her, caressed her, until Katarina hardly knew where she ended and Isaac began.

And that need, that desperate need inside of her was building again.

"You know," Katarina gasped as Isaac's mouth reached one of her nipples, "I used to think that the only way to make love was…you know. How the animals do it."

Isaac broke off his tender ministrations and looked up. "You did?"

Katarina nodded, a little bashfully. "Too much time spent milking cows, I think."

There was a strange look on Isaac's face, one she could not read. Perhaps she would with time, Katarina thought joyfully. Perhaps over time, she would know every inch of him better than she did her own body.

"Do you trust me?" Isaac looked serious, though desire still poured from his eyes.

Katarina nodded. There was no doubt in her mind. "Of course I—Isaac!"

She had squealed just a little, more at the surprise of the movement than anything else. His strong hands had moved to her hips and twisted her. Instead of lying on her back, she was now lying on her front, and Isaac's hands were still on her hips lifting them up, moving her into a sort of crouching position.

Katarina felt the scratch of the hay on her knees and hands, but quite a different feeling quickly eclipsed that. Isaac moved behind her, his manhood grazing her buttocks as his body moved over hers, his hands moving to cup her breasts.

"Oh, Isaac," she murmured, unable to stop herself.

She could not help but cry out his name. Slowly, ever so slowly, but throwing shockwaves of ecstasy through her body that she had never known, Isaac's manhood was slowly entering her from behind. Her secret place quivered as Isaac's hand guided himself in.

Katarina knew now why he had told her to arch her back. It felt wonderful, him filling her from this direction, who knew there could be so many ways to love? There was so much to explore together, to experience together, and—

"Oh, Isaac," she could not help but whimper, the intensity of the pleasure making her shake. "Oh, like that…"

"Kat, I love you," groaned Isaac as he sunk into her once more, the pace quickening. "I love you. I love you—"

"I love you," Katarina almost sobbed, the intensity of her senses almost too much. "Yes, yes, Isaac!"

They reached the pinnacle together, cresting that wave, unable to help themselves crying out in sweet relief, and this time Isaac caught Katarina before she could fall, exhausted, into the hay below her.

She lay nestled in his arms for several minutes, panting, no other thought but to luxuriate in the pleasure they had found.

Eventually, Katarina smiled and pushed back her hair. "That…that was…"

"I hoped you would not mind something a little different," murmured Isaac, lying on his back with his eyes closed.

Katarina laughed. "Mind? If that's what lovemaking is in a cowshed, imagine what it will be like in a bed!"

Isaac chuckled at that, and Katarina kissed him briefly on the cheek before settling back in his arms. Where she belonged. Where she would always be for the rest of their lives.

About Emily E K Murdoch

If you love falling in love, then you've come to the right place.

I am a historian and writer and have a varied career to date: from examining medieval manuscripts to designing museum exhibitions, to working as a researcher for the BBC to working for the National Trust.

My books range from England 1050 to Texas 1848, and I can't wait for you to fall in love with my heroes and heroines!

Follow me on twitter and instagram @emilyekmurdoch, find me on facebook at facebook.com/theemilyekmurdoch, and read my blog at www.emilyekmurdoch.com.

9 781958 098783